Fear Round About

As Beesley turned to leave the ruins behind him, he grew alert again, stiffened and listened. The hair rose on the back of his neck and then he realised that this was no ghostly noise. Someone was digging in the garden at the side of the house, a few acres of ground formerly used for raising vegetables and flowers. In its better days it had been protected by thick box hedges and hazel trees, but now they had degenerated into an almost impassable barrier and the beds were smothered in grass and weeds.

Beesley tiptoed silently across the cobbled yard in the direction of the sound and at length made out a light shining dimly through the bushes. It came from a storm lantern standing on the ground which dimly illuminated a kneeling figure busily exploring a hole he had dug in the soil. As Beesley watched, the man found what he had been seeking and drew it from the earth. It was an object wrapped up in cloth which the intruder eagerly removed. Beesley strained his eyes to identify it and finally succeeded. It was a double-barrelled shotgun.

Other titles in the Walker British Mystery Series

GEORGE BELLAIRS
Fear Round About

WALKER AND COMPANY · NEW YORK

This is a work of fiction, the characters are entirely imaginary, and no reference is made or intended to any person, alive or dead.

First published in the United States of America in 1981 by the Walker Publishing Company, Inc.

This paperback edition first published in 1985.

ISBN: 0-8027-3120-1

Library of Congress Catalog Card Number: 80-54821

Printed in the United States of America

10 9 8 7 6 5 4 3 2 1

Contents

I

The End of Sebastian Dommett

EVERY MORNING before opening the private letters waiting on his desk at Scotland Yard, Littlejohn thumbed through them and tried to guess from the handwriting and postmarks who had sent each of them. It was like a game he played and he felt mild satisfaction whenever he scored a hit. On this Saturday morning, however, there was no doubt about which envelope he opened first. It was on the top of the pile and addressed in a bold hand with heavy downstrokes, as though the writer had used a quill pen. It was post-marked Aylesdon on the previous day.

Littlejohn was completely baffled by it and slit the envelope immediately. It contained a single sheet of paper with a few lines in the same aggressive script. It was addressed from *The Stables, Swinton Lazars, Midshire.*

Dear Littlejohn,

    I am told that you are retiring in six months' time and have a proposition to make to you. Please call to see me here some time soon but warn me by telephone when you will arrive.

                    Yours,

                    Sebastian Dommett.

Sebastian Dommett! Littlejohn sat back in his chair staring at the letter in jet black ink. Before his retirement, about seven years ago, Dommett had been County Coroner for Downshire, and he and the Chief Superintendent had, during his term of office, met several times in his court. He had conducted his inquiries like a high court judge and since his daughter had eloped with a police constable, had developed an aversion to the police which he manifested publicly whenever he could.

The Stables. That was like Dommett, too. He was always complaining about being underpaid and not being able to make ends meet on his salary. The address was like a charade advertising the depths to which he had sunk on his miserable pension.

Littlejohn remembered him best in his prime. A tall, lean, dark and bitter man, who in those days had worn a large moustache with pointed waxed ends, and he went about his business like a bleak shadow. He was accompanied by two assistants, Bugler and Waddilove, known familiarly to the police as Tweedledee and Tweedledum. They had been part of his retinue since a demented witness had attacked Dommett and given him a black eye and a damaged nose, with which he remained in bed until all traces of the fracas had disappeared.

Littlejohn wondered whence Dommett had gathered the news of his retirement, which, as yet, had not been settled or noised around. He and Letty had been casually making up their minds recently about where they were going to live and now and then superficially inspecting odd places and properties. Perhaps Dommett had a house for sale. In any case it would be another outing. Littlejohn reached for the Gazetteer.

Swinton Lazars was in the Midlands between Market Storton and Midchester and, according to the Gazetteer, as its name implied, had been the site of a large monastic leper hospital in the middle ages, but of which there was now no trace. Population, blank. One pub., the *Antelope*. Distance from London, 82¾ miles.

As far as possible, the Littlejohns had avoided exploring for their retirement at week-ends, when roads were choked with excursionists, and estate agents and property owners were peevish when their Saturdays and Sundays were intruded upon. However, Mr. Dommett had made no reservations about dates when he issued the invitation and his letter had a measure of urgency about it. Littlejohn rang up his wife and they arranged to leave at noon that day for Swinton Lazars. Letty promised to bring sandwiches and coffee for lunch. It was a bright early autumn morning and lunch in the country on the way instead of in haste at one of the busy hotels seemed a better idea.

There was a telephone number on the notepaper and Littlejohn asked the switchboard operator to get it. As he waited for the call he wondered how time had dealt with Sebastian Dommett. The last time they had met had been more than ten years ago in the Stainton Meredith murders and they had not got on very well together. It was shortly after Dommett's daughter had run away with the local constable and he was on the prowl for unwary policemen on whom to vent his spleen. Dommett was a pompous and

meddlesome man and his inquests had always taken twice
as much time as was necessary.

Telephone. A woman's voice answered from the other end.

' Is that Mrs. Dommett?'

' Mr. Dommett's wife died three years ago . . .'

There was a rebuke in the voice.

' This is his housekeeper. Who is that?'

Littlejohn told her and mentioned the letter.

' He is out at present. Can I give him a message?'

The tone was cautious, to say the least of it. There was
a protective inflexion, as though Littlejohn was going to do
some harm to Dommett.

' No, thank you. I'll ring again. What time will be
convenient?'

The woman did not reply. There was silence and Littlejohn thought for a minute that the line had gone dead. He
was just going to hang up when there was a sound like a
sigh at the other end and then whispering.

' Who is it?'

This time it was a man's voice.

Littlejohn had made one mistake about the late Mrs.
Dommett. Besides, the voice wasn't the old familiar rasping
one of long-ago coroner's inquests.

' May I ask if Mr. Dommett is at home?'

' This *is* Mr. Dommett! Who are you?'

' Chief Superintendant Littlejohn . . .'

' Why didn't you give your name to my housekeeper when
you spoke to her?'

' I did give her my name . . .'

' She's a bit deaf. You should have shouted . . .'

This was more like the old Dommett. Squabbling about nothing, even when he was in the wrong!

' I was not expecting you so soon . . .'

They did not seem to be making much progress. Littlejohn wondered if he had better make an excuse and let the matter drop. After all, what did Dommett want with him after his retirement and what did he want with Dommett, the scourge of policemen? He couldn't imagine anything more boring and unpleasant than the company of the superannuated coroner.

' Are you there, Littlejohn? You've decided to talk over the matter about which I wrote to you?'

' You didn't mention what it was . . .'

' Later. I certainly don't wish to discuss it over the telephone. When can you come?'

' We are free this afternoon.'

' We? This is a matter for yourself alone.'

' I propose to bring my wife with me. Anything concerning my retirement is shared with her.'

' Very well. You were always a stubborn man, Littlejohn. The sooner we have a talk the better. We'll say four o'clock then. Come for tea.'

' Thank you sir.'

' Good day, then. Ask anyone in Swinton where I live. They'll show you the way.'

Dommett hung up without more ado.

Letty joined Littlejohn in London at noon and they started on their way to the Midlands. It was a warm sunny day and they drove leisurely along quiet roads avoiding the motorways. They ate lunch near Market Storton, looked at the shops there, and then made for Swinton Lazars.

'Swinton Lazars?' said the inspector at the bus station, when they asked him for precise directions. 'Swinton Lazars . . . You'll be lucky, sir. It's a deserted village. Nobody lives there, although it's a nice spot for a Sunday outing. There's quite a lot of places like that round here. It's as if the inhabitants had suddenly all decided to pack up and leave.'

They thanked him, feeling more confused than ever, and decided to follow the map. Littlejohn, whose duties had brought him several times into the locality, had grown to admire the unspectacular beauty of High Midshire, with its quiet villages, quaint churches and attractive stretches of peaceful pastoral countryside. According to Mrs. Littlejohn's hasty researches, Swinton Lazars was a small village astride the now-forsaken Roman Gartree road in the triangle of country between Midchester city, Market Storton and Aylesdon.

A deserted village! Nobody there! It was like Sebastian Dommett to advise him to ask anyone where he lived, when there was nobody to ask!

The countryside was gently undulating and the secondary road followed its contours up and down. There was a profusion of sign-posts along the way from Market Storton, sign-posts bearing graceful double-barrelled names like Kidlington Curlieu, Ashby Harcourt, Cold Barsby . . .

They asked the way once or twice as they went along. Swinton Lazars . . . People seemed surprised that they should want to go to such a place. They looked sheepish and frightened at the mention of the name, as though

Swinton were still the lepers' village and to be shunned.

At Cold Barsby, with tremendous views northward over the Trent Valley, on top of a hill and hence presumably its name, there was an inn and a few cottages, with a stumpy old church and a large house, obviously the vicarage, huddled in a clump of trees behind. At one time or another it had been a larger community judging from the size of the church and the relics of former dwellings. As in many other places in the vicinity, practically the whole of the population had migrated elsewhere where earnings were better and amenities up-to-date.

There was a moth-eaten village green stretching before the village pub and it was a scene of considerable activity. A crowd of excited people was milling about round stalls and marquees and trying skills at fairground games of every kind. A small brass quartet was enthusiastically playing 'Summer Gardens' out of tune and the Cold Barsby country dancers were clapping hands and capering about. In a nearby field a sack race was in progress amid the encouraging shouts of the spectators, and the handbell ringers were lined up for a performance. The Littlejohns had plenty of time to spare and were almost at the end of their journey, so they stopped on the edge of the green, dismounted and joined the revellers.

Their unexpected arrival there came as a surprise and caused a brief pause in the proceedings, which were slowly resumed after word had gone round that they were casual travellers and not local gentry calling to patronise the event. The vicar, however, was determined to know a little more about the visitors. He emerged from the tea tent, a cup of tea trembling in each hand, and approached them.

' May I offer you a cup of tea on this thirsty afternoon?'

Littlejohn insisted on paying for the treat and the vicar persisted on remaining in conversation. He was an aged man, but still vigorous. Dressed in shabby black, with traces of food down the front of his long out-of-date coat and wearing an old-fashioned hat, he looked like an ancient Vicar of Wakefield who had wandered in from the distant past. He had a shock of grey hair, dishevelled by the tireless wind of Cold Barsby, and the chubby red face and corpulent figure of one who enjoyed high living.

' Welcome to our little celebration,' he said. ' It is saint's day at our church and we hold an annual feast in his honour and to raise funds for his church. In the past it was a very famous event in these parts. People flocked here from miles around, even from as far as Midchester and Market Storton . . .'

He paused and shrugged his shoulders cheerfully as though the change didn't matter much.

' Are you going far?' he asked them.

' Just to Swinton Lazars. I believe it isn't far from here.'

The curiosity and sparkle died from the old man's eyes, as though he had been in the world of time and space too long and was eager to return within himself.

Mrs. Littlejohn excused herself and left them to talk and circulated among the crowd, patronising the sellers of homemade confections and from the white elephant stall she bought a Staffordshire figure which must have been a collector's treasure at some time and which, to her, made the long journey worth while.

The vicar recovered from his surprise at Littlejohn's destination and, having broken the ice, he pursued his inquiries.

'Had you any purpose in visiting Swinton? It is a deserted place with little worth seeing except a lot of ruins.'

'We are calling to see Mr. Dommett, who, I understand, has retired there.'

'I know of Mr. Dommett. I am incumbent of the two parishes of Cold Barsby and Swinton Lazars. There is a church at Swinton, but I attend there only about a once a fortnight. There is no congregation and the fabric is badly in need of repair. As for Mr. Dommett . . .'

The old man sighed. 'He does not welcome visitors. He was formerly a county coroner of Downshire and retired to Swinton some years ago. Is he a friend or relative of yours?'

The vicar's discourse was rambling and he paused now and then to gather his thoughts together. He had many worries. On top of his anxieties about the funds to be raised from the effort now in progress, he had two decaying parishes in his care and he had married late in life a young woman who had borne him five children, and he was therefore heavily involved in domesticity as well as religious labours.

'As for Mr. Dommett . . . When he arrived in Swinton Lazars I endeavoured to call on him. His wife had inherited the old manor house there and he began by encircling it with a stout wire fence. When I appeared at the gate I was confronted by a large fierce dog, which bared its teeth in a terrifying manner. It was followed by Mr. Dommett, who did not admit me, but told me he was an atheist and had no need of my ministrations. I was greatly perturbed. It was bad having a godless unbeliever in the parish, because relations between the church and the manor house had always, in the past, been most cordial and the occupants had always treated us most generously. In fact, the residents in the manor house owned a large private pew in the church . . . If you are calling on Mr. Dommett, beware of the dog.'

'Is he the sole remaining resident in the village?'

'Two other small houses there are occupied by old people who were born there, and are not likely to remove except in death. The rest of the dwellings are either empty and rapidly decaying, or else are used as week-end cottages for dwellers in nearby towns who come there for a few days in the country and then shut them up again until their next visit. That is a frequent habit in the locality. The former inhabitants of one-time agricultural villages here have gone to the towns to improve their incomes and enjoy the facilities of town life. These villages are dead or dying. Another few years and they will be completely deserted and forlorn.'

The interview was terminated by the arrival of a panting fat lady who hung around until the vicar became aware of her presence.

'Hello, Mrs. Seal . . .'

'We've run out of tea, Mr. Beecham. Could Mrs. Beecham let us have half a pound? We'll pay her back.'

'Excuse me . . .'

The vicar bustled off in the direction of the vicarage, followed by his wobbling parishioner. Once home again the good man must have become involved in domestic affairs, for Littlejohn did not see him again.

The Littlejohns continued on their way. Hardly a vehicle passed them between the two villages. A sign-post or two, *Kings Kilby*, *Little Carlton*, *Burton Masterton*, melodious double-barrelled places, but Swinton Lazars never appeared there. The road was straight and descended slowly from Cold Barsby and then maintained its level after that. In ten minutes they reached their destination. A one-armed sign-post stood at the side of the highway at the end of the by-road which led to Swinton, the name of which was not on it, however, as though it urged the traveller to avoid the place and go to *Ashby Newbold* instead.

The by-way ran straight through the village and ended in a cul-de-sac. Near the end, the road widened out in a small square of about a dozen houses built of stone, some in terraces. Several of them were in ruins with only their walls standing. The rest were apparently owned by week-enders and had been renovated and painted-up. They were all locked and some of them shuttered. Although it was week-end, there was nobody about. An empty horse trough stood in one corner of the square and on one side the church, cold and locked up, under a disorderly canopy of old elms and yew trees.

The *Antelope* inn, scheduled in the guide book, was in order, but closed. Later, Littlejohn learned that it had been bought by a wealthy land speculator who used it for entertaining his private guests.

Somewhere a clock struck four in muffled tones, the last note of which hung reluctantly on the air and slowly faded away. There was evidently someone living among the accumulation of decaying houses. There was a scent of wood smoke, too, which confirmed the impression.

The Littlejohns instinctively walked quietly about the place, almost on tiptoes, and without exchanging a word, as though afraid to awake the dead or disturb the tranquillity of the few remaining occupants who seemed to be hiding from view. The soft chiming of the clock reminded them they were there to see Dommett at 4 p.m. Littlejohn checked it by his watch. It was 3.50.

'Where's the manor house and stables?' said Littlejohn in a whisper, as though to himself.

It was not visible and there was nobody about to show them the way. The visitors, under the melancholy weight of the forlorn village, grew eager to meet Dommett, hear what he had to say, and then hurry away. The atmosphere was suddenly relieved by the arrival of a bustling Post Office van, which came to a halt opposite the horse trough. The engine stopped and a postman, chubby, red haired and with elaborate sideburns growing on his cheeks, climbed out. He was whistling, but his tune came to a sudden stop when he saw the visitors, who felt like trespassers there.

'Good afternoon,' he shouted at them and paused, waiting for them to say something in reply. They returned his greeting and joined him.

'What brings you to this god-forsaken place?'

'We're trying to find the manor house, where Mr. Dommett lives. The place seems deserted and we were just seeking someone to tell us where it is. Is there anyone living here?'

' Two of the houses are occupied by old people. The rest went one by one. There's nothing here to stay for. It's dead. I've come all the way from Aylesdon to deliver a circular to Mr. Dommett and a letter from the Social Security for the Pepperdys. You want the manor house . . . ?'

He pointed at a clump of trees and bushes beyond the cul-de-sac.

'The house is among that lot. At one time you could see it from here, but the spinney has been allowed to grow wild and the whole place is neglected. Old Dommett, the occupier, is a crank. A bit potty, if you ask me. He moved in here before my time, but from what I hear his wife inherited the property. She was the last of the Mowll family, they say. Died about three years ago. They made the stables into a residence when they moved in and left the manor house to rot. I believe he talked once of making flats of the big house, but must have thought better of it. Nobody would want to move into this tumbledown place.'

' Are you calling at the manor with letters?'

' As I said, I've a letter here for the Pepperdys and then I'll be going there with this circular. A waste of time. I'll show you the way, if you'll wait a minute. Is he expecting you? If he isn't, you'll be lucky if he lets you anywhere near the place. He lives there alone, with a housekeeper and a chap who's a sort of butler and handyman and another who does a bit of gardening. I'll just deliver this . . .'

He left them and disappeared round the corner of one of the ruined houses. The place was completely silent and they could hear him knocking at a door and then greeting and asking about the health of the occupiers.

He was absent for some time and when he returned excused himself for keeping them waiting.

'The Pepperdys are both turned 80 and have lived here most of their lives. There's another family, too, on the other side of the village. Old folks who'd die if they were up-rooted. I've just taken the Pepperdys a form for claiming their old age pension. One can't read, and the other can't understand what the form is all about and I've had to help them fill it in and then they put their crosses to it and I witnessed it. Now I'm taking it back with me. It's pathetic. All the lot of them ought to be in old people's homes, but they won't go. I keep telling them it's not like the old-fashioned workhouses, but they'd rather end their lives in this dump, sitting by the fire dreaming the days away . . . Let's go.'

He brightened up and began to whistle again under his breath.

It was half-past four and Littlejohn looked anxiously at his watch. The postman noticed the gesture but said noth-ing, then:

'You've got your car, I see. We'd better go to the front entrance. There's a field path from here. I use it now and then when I've time to spare, but you want to be getting there, so we'll go back to the main road. Follow me . . .'

He sprang in his van and led the way back to the high-way. They followed the postal van for about half a mile and then it halted before a rusty iron gate. The postman descended and opened it with some difficulty, for it was askew and sunk in the earth at one end. A long neglected drive led to another clump of trees and shrubs, beyond which they could see the chimneys of Dommett's strange dwelling which, as they approached it, gradually revealed itself.

Finally, another gate.

'This is where I leave you, sir,' said the cheerful postman. There was a metal box, fitted with a lock, fixed to the post at the side of the gate and labelled 'POST'. The postman slipped his envelope in the slit on the top of the box.

'They don't like visitors here,' he said. 'Not even the postman. You go on from here, sir, till you reach a sort of wicket gate. There's a wire fence there and the gate is in the middle of it. There's a bell hanging. You ring that. The gate is locked and if they're in a good mood when you ring they'll come to see what you want. Don't try to get in until somebody comes. There's a dog loose there and it's not safe . . .'

They thanked the postman and he wished them good luck and left them.

They got the impression that he was sorry for them and, as the red van turned into the highway and disappeared and silence fell again, they seemed to be left in a strange realm of fantasy and spells, like a theatre set ready for a nightmare.

They parked the car and made their way in the direction of the wicket gate, through a tunnel of unkempt trees and tangled undergrowth. The view of the manor house gradually unfolded, revealing a motley group of buildings set in a wilderness of grass, once presumably a lawn, now untidy and overgrown.

The Littlejohns said little to each other. Each knew what

the other was thinking. They were tired and disappointed
and it would have needed very little to persuade them to
abandon the whole fantastic adventure and return home to
familiar places and people.

Littlejohn was just about to suggest it, when he halted in
his tracks. They had been walking hand in hand in mutual
comfort and understanding. Now Littlejohn left his wife.

' Just stay where you are, Letty.'

He hurried over the rough ground on the side of the
neglected drive towards one of the large ivy-covered trees
in the wilderness of the spinney. At the foot of the trunk lay
an untidy bundle which he instinctively knew was to be the
climax of the whole sorry affair.

It was the body of a man in a heavy overcoat, turned
face downwards in a mass of dead leaves and twigs of many
a past autumn. His hat lay some distance away and on the
back of his head a mass of congealed blood covered a
savage wound. Littlejohn stood with his hands on his
hips contemplating his find for a moment. His wife joined
him.

' What is it?'

Littlejohn turned the body over. They both gasped with
horror. It was that of an old man with an untidy grey
beard. The face was soiled and the mouth was full of dead
leaves and earth, as though the victim had convulsively
bitten into the ground in the agony of death. There were
signs of a struggle on the surrounding turf. At first Littlejohn failed to recognise the features, then mentally stripped
them of beard and disfigurement.

It was the body of Mr. Sebastian Dommett.

2

The House at Swinton Lazars

MR. SEBASTIAN DOMMETT had been an awkward man in life and his death was equally awkward. The first thing Littlejohn had to do was to sound the alarm. Having made quite sure the man was dead, he and his wife turned to the wicket gate in the fence. The bell was there, mounted on a stout post. It resembled a miniature ship's bell with a rope hanging from the clapper. Littlejohn rang it vigorously. Almost at once, from somewhere among the buildings a large Alsatian dog appeared, bounded to the fence, bared his teeth and snarled. Nobody else responded. As the note of the bell died away a sad profound silence fell over the place again. Even the rooks in the trees above, which had been agitated by the sudden disturbance and chattered excitedly, grew quiet.

The manor house had come into full view. It was in ruins and abandoned. A seventeenth century brick building, consisting of a main structure with a wing on each side, with large stone-framed bay windows. The glass in the small-paned windows was broken and the low brick wall surrounding the front was tumbledown with ivy romping all over it. On one side a walled garden overgrown with tall weeds, and in it Littlejohn made out the heavy protruding rump of a large figure apparently setting out bedding plants in a small square of earth carved out of the ruin of the place. The man had not heeded the bell or the furious barking of the dog and a further ring had no effect. Littlejohn shouted as loudly as he could but was ignored. It was only when the gardener slowly rose to ease his back that he saw the visitors. He seemed surprised to see them, but quite unimpressed and shambled across the neglected lawn and joined them. 'Is anyone at home?' said Littlejohn.

The man looked at him blankly. He had a heavy expressionless face with drooling lips, and one eye seemed sightless. He pointed to his ears.

'Deaf. Speak up'

Meanwhile the dog kept up his barking and snarling.

'Sharrup!' the deaf man said to him and raised the hoe he was carrying. The dog, which must have suffered from the implement in the past, gave it a single alarmed look and made off yelping and vanished among the ruins.

The wicket gate was locked and Littlejohn signalled to the man to open it. The man shook his head and pointed to the lock. Presumably he hadn't the key. To the astonishment of the gardener, Littlejohn raised his foot and kicked off the hasp.

'I want the telephone . . .'

The gardener was at a loss but showed no sign of resistance.

'You can't . . .'

'Telephone?' shouted Littlejohn, pointing to the overhead wires which crossed the front of the house and vanished among the other buildings in the rear of it. The Littlejohns followed the line of the wires and the gardener seemed content to shuffle after them. He was talking to himself.

'Mr. Dommett won't like it. He'll be mad at you,' he said and he seemed to have settled in his mind how the intrusion would end.

'Where's the housekeeper?' bawled Littlejohn.

This time the question seemed to penetrate.

'Gone to Aylesdon to the shops.'

The Littlejohns followed the trail of the telephone cable which led them across a square cobbled courtyard, untended, bristling with grass growing between the stones. The yard was surrounded by buildings embracing one side of the ruined house and the remaining three sides consisted of brick outhouses which must at one time have been extensive barns, coach houses and stables but which now were tumbledown and neglected. The present residential part stood out in better trim than the rest. The one-time blank walls of one of the stables had been broken by sash windows and a substantial door added. The place seemed deserted.

The deaf gardener, who had shuffled along a few paces behind the Littlejohns, pointed to the lock in the door and made a hopeless gesture to indicate that he hadn't a key. Littlejohn looked in at one of the windows. The room was large and dark but on a desk under the window the telephone was visible among a confusion of books, papers and writing materials. Mrs. Littlejohn, at his elbow, seemed more impressed by the living quarters than elsewhere.

'It looks a bit more cosy inside, but there must be a lot of rats and other vermin about . . .'

And, as though to confirm it, a large rat crossed the yard. It ignored the intruders completely and seemed intent on its own business.

All the windows in the frontage were fastened. The gable-end round the corner was bare of any openings whatever and they moved to the back, the gardener following them with his large moon face as blank as the brick wall. Now and then he uttered a single word as something or other sank into his consciousness.

The back of the building was neglected like the rest of the surroundings, and in an enclosure constructed of heavy wire, the rubbish of years had accumulated; dustbins filled to overflowing, an incinerator packed with burnt paper, a rusty old lawn mower and a garden roller and some broken chairs. In one corner, a wooden shed with a broken hinge and the door askew. There were rich crops of nettles growing along the bottom of the enclosure which might have been a flooded part of the drainage system.

‘ Nettles,’ said the gardener as though he had just become aware of their existence.

There were three windows on the ground floor, all secured by modern catches. There was nothing else for it; Little-john, with a piece of rusty iron from a pile of scrap, broke one of the small panes of the window nearest the back door, thrust back the fastening and with difficulty opened the window and clambered in.

The gardener’s eyes grew round with wonder and he extended his vocabulary in protest.

‘ Mr. Dommett won’t like that . . .’

On the inside, Littlejohn landed with his feet in a well-cleaned porcelain sink. Unlike the exterior of the place, this room, which must have been the kitchen, was scrupulously tidy and polished and was obviously the quarters of a housekeeper who was more conscientious about her duties than the outdoor staff. A large plain-wood kitchen table dominated the floor, with four cottage chairs and a well-tended welsh dresser with porcelain plates and pewter vessels scattered about the shelves. In one corner a heavy black oak door led into the front room already briefly inspected by the Littlejohns through the window. It was as neat and tidy as the kitchen and judging from the furniture must have been the living room. Littlejohn had little inclination to conduct a further inspection. He left that to his wife, whom he admitted by unbarring the back door. Then, with the impression foremost in his mind of Dommett lying dead among the soil and withered leaves of the spinney, he hurried across the room and picked up the telephone.

Littlejohn had no idea by which police district the deserted village was controlled, but he thought immediately of Frank Winstanley, Chief Superintendent of the C.I.D in Midshire County, which probably exercised jurisdiction in that part of the world. He dialled three nines and at first found himself being informed by the telephonic time-clock that at the third stroke it would be five-thirty-four precisely. He tried again and this time was put through to the county police headquarters, waiting for Chief Superintendent Winstanley.

Winstanley and Littlejohn were old colleagues and had worked together at Scotland Yard until Winstanley had left for a better job in the Midlands. Luckily, he was in his office and was pleasantly surprised to hear from his old friend again.

'Where are you ringing from?' asked Winstanley after an exchange of greetings.

'The stables of the manor house at Swinton Lazars . . .'

'What the hell are you doing there? Not visiting old Dommett, are you? He seems to be the only one alive in that god-forsaken place.'

'I came here to visit him, but I found him dead in the adjacent spinney. I wondered if this was your territory and would you take over from me . . .'

'Well, well. Yes; it's under our control. I'd better come and join you there right away. It will take me half-an-hour to get there. Do you suspect foul play?'

'No doubt about it. There's a nasty blow on the back of his head. He must have been knocked down from behind. I left him just as I found him and went to the nearest phone, which is in the stables of the manor house where Dommett lived. I'll wait for you and we'll talk when you arrive . . .'

There seemed to be little to do now but wait for Winstanley. Littlejohn felt averse to prowling about the place, although he was greatly tempted. He was like a trespasser, which indeed he was; breaking into Dommett's house was quite enough without intruding on Winstanley's pitch. He and his wife decided to wait and found themselves chairs in the living room. The hush of death seemed to have descended on the place and their conversation became monosyllabic. Their thoughts seemed to be of Dommett, dead and past helping, lying among mould in the spinney, waiting for the local police and technicians to find him a decent resting-place after they'd finished with him.

The quiet was not maintained for long. A small car labelled POLICE appeared at the gap in the hedge at which Littlejohn had made his violent entry and a burly policeman, all spick and span, gloved and with bright boots, stepped out, examined the broken gate perfunctorily, looked around to take his bearings and then marched across to the house. Littlejohn followed his course through the window. A well-built, ruddy country constable in his early forties. Surely, he thought, I've met that chap elsewhere at some time or other.

The bobby entered by the front door which Littlejohn had unfastened for him. He faced Littlejohn a bit self-consciously and with a broad smile on his face. He saluted smartly.

' Chief Superintendent Winstanley told me to report to you here, sir . . .'

' Wait. I've met you somewhere before . . .'

Littlejohn rummaged among past memories, trying to extricate the real individual from the one which time had so much altered. The constable could not wait for the riddle to be solved.

' Charlie Sadd,' he said.

The official barrier between them and the formalities of their discipline melted away and they shook hands cordially. Littlejohn introduced his wife.

' This is Charlie Sadd, Letty. He was a lad of about 15 last time we met. His father was resident constable in Stainton Meredith when I was there on a murder case and Charlie was the terror of the girls of the village . . .'

' I'm married now, and three kids,' said Charlie by way of assuring them that he had mended his ways.

' How is your father, Charlie?'

' He was 80 last Easter and fit and well, thank you. He still lives at Stainton with mother, who's 81, and well. I'm living at Nether Bleasby, four miles from here on the Kings Melton side . . .'

' I suppose the Chief Superintendent has told you what has happened. Mr. Sebastian Dommett has been murdered and his body is lying in the spinney near the side entrance to the hall. I've left everything as we found it. I suppose you knew Mr. Dommett, Charlie.'

' Yes, sir. I remember him from the old days when he used to come to Stainton from time to time. Father didn't like him. Said he was a bully. He was always accompanied by two men they called his watchdogs . . .'

' And you've had nothing to do with him since those days?'

' I've been called in here a time or two. Mr. Dommett complained about the vandals — youths who raced about the countryside on motor-bikes — damaging or destroying anything they came across. You can see from the ruin of this place what a temptation it must be to such rabble to ruin it more. And then there's a deserted village, Swinton Lazars, just across the fields there. Gangs of men and boys on motor-bikes invade the place now and then, breaking in the unoccupied houses and smashing windows. Every time there was a visit from the vandals, Mr. Dommett was on the phone to us, blaming us for lack of vigilance, as if we could do anything. By the time we got here, the damage was done and the birds had flown. Mr. Dommett fired a shotgun at one lot of youths. We had to reprimand him for that. As a retired county coroner he ought to have known better. A good job he didn't hit any of them.

They got no further, for there was another intrusion. At the first sound of a car along the neglected drive they thought it was Winstanley and his retinue arriving, but it turned out to be an old taxi driven by a man who crouched over the wheel as though it was his sole means of support. Inside the vehicle they could dimly see a dark form clad in black relieved by a purple jumper. The dilapidated cab halted at the damaged gate and the driver remained at his seat like one in a trance until his passenger scrambled out. The broken lock at once caught her eye and forgetting that she hadn't paid her fare she rushed to examine the damage.

'Who's done this?' she said in an angry voice. She looked so agitated that she might have fainted or suffered a stroke at any minute.

The driver was affronted.

'Don't ask me. I couldn't care less. All I know is you've not paid your fare and I'm in a hurry.'

The woman returned to the taxi and dragged out two bulky shopping bags overflowing with provisions, as though the manor was about to resist a siege. From one of these she produced a handbag out of which she took a purse and counted out coins in the driver's extended palm. The driver continued to extend his hand after she had paid her dues, but the woman ignored it. Finding no tip forthcoming, the man turned his vehicle and drove off.

The woman examined the damage at the gate again and then gathering her bags made for the house at a shambling trot. P.C. Sadd opened the front door to receive her. She gave a startled cry.

'You frightened me! What are you doing here and who let you in?'

Without waiting for an answer she brushed past the bobby and entered the room.

'Where is Mr. Dommett?' she said as she passed Sadd. Then she saw the Littlejohns standing on the hearthrug.

'Who are you? What are you doing here?'

Sadd, following on her heels, introduced the Littlejohns.

'I knew they were coming, but where's Mr. Dommett?' She stood tense and angry glaring from one to another.

P.C. Sadd raised his hand like a parson pronouncing a benediction.

'Don't get so excited, Mrs. Batt. I'll tell you what it's all about if you'll only listen. Mr. Dommett has had an accident.'

One could imagine Sadd adopting the same tone and address when he spoke to his children when they were in trouble.

'Where is he? Is it bad? Is he in bed?'

'I'm sorry to say, Mrs. Batt, that Mr. Dommett is dead. His body's lying in the spinney by the drive and we are waiting for the police to come from Midchester and deal with it.'

Mrs. Batt stood wild-eyed and petrified for a minute and then burst out hysterically.

'He died and you've left him there without anybody to

watch over his dead body. I'm going to him. I'm not afraid of death if you are.'

She had taken off her hat and now she put it on again hastily and awry. It gave her a rakish expression. Charlie Sadd remained unperturbed. He raised his hand again.

'You can't go there at present, Mrs. Batt. Nobody's allowed there until the police arrive to photograph and examine the corpse. Now just calm down. We'll see to everything. Go into the kitchen with Mrs. Littlejohn and make yourselves a nice cup of tea.'

Mrs. Littlejohn smiled at Charlie's manoeuvring and put an arm round Mrs. Batt's shoulders.

'Come along, Mrs. Batt, and I'll tell you all about it over a cup of tea.'

The gesture released her suppressed shock and Mrs. Batt buried her face in Letty's shoulder and sobbed loudly. Then she began a plaintive chattering. They couldn't tell what it was all about, but Dommett was included in it. Mrs. Littlejohn led her away to the kitchen.

After this interlude the Midchester police arrived in two vehicles. Winstanley was with them and greeted Littlejohn boisterously, as if they were meeting at a wedding instead of a violent death. He was a large cheerful officer with a refined easy manner, often misunderstood by offenders until it was too late.

Sadd, who had, in the circumstances, taken temporary charge, then withdrew and resumed his constabulary place and deference and left to Littlejohn the details of what had happened hitherto and how he had got mixed up in the affair.

'We'd better go across and see the body, then,' said Winstanley. 'I wish we were working together on this case, Tom, like we often used to do. You didn't examine the body . . .?'

'No. The spot is remote and it was unlikely that any-body would interfere with it. First and foremost we had to get hold of you as quickly as possible. There was nobody about but a deaf, half-witted gardener. So I acted as I thought fit.'

Back at the scene of the murder the atmosphere had changed from one of melancholy and gloom to businesslike activity. Technicians of various kinds were busy about their duties, chatting, comparing notes and even laughing and joking with one another. The doctor had arrived, too, and after a cursory examination of the body had turned it over to the technical staff who were moving it to a waiting ambulance.

'Death due to a blow on the head which damaged the brain. Provisionally, I'd say he died between ten o'clock and noon, but that will have to be confirmed later . . .'

Photographs were taken of the site, the locality searched. Some of the officers were busy farther afield beating the bushes and hunting for the murder weapon. Overhead, the colony of rooks, disturbed by the commotion below, were cawing and flapping their wings.

Littlejohn and Winstanley returned to the house. As they crossed the dilapidated courtyard Winstanley paused, his hands on his hips, and surveyed the scene of ruin which had once been Swinton Lazars Hall.

'It must have been a fine place in its prime. Now, what

a mess. Dommett must just have watched the place falling down. Not the slightest effort made to save it. He probably hadn't the money to spend on it. I wonder why he sent for you, Tom . . .'

'As far as I can guess, he'd heard I was shortly due to retire and wanted either to offer me a job or the tenancy of another part of the outhouses. Knowing Dommett, I wouldn't have been interested in either.'

'What sort of a job?'

'Bodyguard or security officer.'

'You must be joking! One doesn't offer work of that kind to retired top officials of Scotland Yard.'

'I wouldn't put anything past him. Years ago, when last I had anything to do with him, he was a bit crazy. Now, living among this ruin on his own, he might have gone completely off his head.'

'If we find what he was going to offer you, we might be a bit nearer finding his murderer.'

'I'm almost sure he was going to offer me a security job . . .'

'But what does he need security for in all this tumble-down property? You'd think he'd be glad to give it away.'

'Personal security would be what he was after. He was afraid of being attacked, beaten up or murdered. I remember when he was in harness as county coroner, he always travelled about with a couple of sturdy assistants called coroner's officers, but really strong-arm men. He was attacked once and badly mauled. Ever after that his two men were with him. We called them Tweedledee and Tweedledum.'

' I wonder if they're still with him.'

' I doubt it. We'll find out soon enough.'

' You are very much involved in this case, Tom. You found the body and were here to meet Dommett about something neither of us knows anything about. You knew him and his background. You'd be a great help. Why not stay and give us some assistance with the case? You and I could work together ...'

Winstanley seemed determined to put the clock back and include Littlejohn in the team, as they'd done long ago.

' It's tempting, Frank. But we didn't come here intending to stay even overnight. I'll tell you what we'll do. My wife and I will return to London tonight and I'll come down here by train first thing in the morning. It's only about an hour's journey in the fast train to and from Midchester.'

' Right. I'll see to the formalities with Scotland Yard and put things on a proper footing. And now, let's have a word with Mrs. Batt. She's our principal witness.'

When they reached the house, they found Sadd drinking tea and eating scones and talking to Mrs. Littlejohn. Mrs. Batt was nowhere to be seen.

' Mrs. Batt has gone to her room to pack a bag,' explained Mrs. Littlejohn. ' She says on no account will she stay here alone tonight.'

' I don't blame her,' said Winstanley, ' But where does she propose to go?'

' Her sister lives at Burton Masterton, about ten miles away, just off the Market Storton road. She'll need transport, I think. It seems Mr. Dommett used to be absent from time to time in the summer and she always went to stay with her sister then.'

Thereupon Mrs. Batt appeared carrying a suitcase. She was bewildered by the circumstances and very set in her decision to leave almost right away.

She was a tallish, middle-aged woman, dark and good-looking, almost like a gipsy. She arrived talking to herself and when she saw the police there, raised her voice to include them in her complaints. She seemed to be blaming Dommett for her present predicament.

' . . . Never in my worst dreams did I ever think it would come to this. When I left, he was drinking his morning coffee and grumbling as usual. Every morning after he'd read *The Times*, he started to complain about the state of the world. As for staying here the night, I would not if you was to give me a hundred pounds to do it. This place is bad enough, but with that old ruin there . . . it's haunted . . .'

She turned on Sadd, who was smiling as usual.

' And you don't smile, Charlie Sadd. You wouldn't smile if you was to spend a night in that old ruin . . .'

' Mrs. Littlejohn tells me you are going to stay with your sister for the time being. P.C. Sadd will take you to Burton,' said Winstanley.

She seemed relieved.

' The sooner the better. Is his corpse still in the wood?'

' It's been moved to Midchester.'

Mrs. Batt seemed to have recovered her equilibrium. No tears or hysterics. She was taking matters as they came and looking after her own interests.

'Shall we be getting off to Burton, then? There's not much I can do here, is there?'

'We'll want to ask you some questions first, Mrs. Batt.'

'I don't know anything about it. He was all right when I set out to Aylesdon to do my shopping. Ten o'clock, that was.'

'And you left him indoors, drinking his coffee.'

'That's right, as I said before. I've a good idea who killed him, too.'

'Who?'

'The gipsies, of course. They're all over the place. There's always a crowd of them camping round the Gartree road. They were always sneaking around here and the village, seeing what they could steal. Mr. Dommett took his gun to them once or twice. I'm sure it's one of them who did it.'

'Have there been any of them about lately?'

'Yes. One called last week to ask if they could put their caravan in the paddock by the road. Mr. Dommett told him no they couldn't and if he saw them about again he'd put the police on them.'

'And the gipsy cleared off without an argument.'

'Yes. Except as he turned to go the gipsy said he'd regret it and he wouldn't forget.'

3

A Broken Partnership

Mrs. Littlejohn, anticipating that proceedings were likely to become protracted, had already arranged with Mrs. Batt for refreshments of one sort or another to be served.

'There doesn't seem to be a place where one can eat in this locality,' she said to Mrs. Batt. 'I'm sure the men will need a meal as they'll probably be here for some time yet. Can you and I find something . . .?'

Mrs. Batt had proved very co-operative. She had taken a fancy to Mrs. Littlejohn and while the men were absent had taken her into her confidence about her life with the late Mr. Batt, who had died of a heart attack shortly after their marriage, and Mr. Sebastian Dommett and other personal matters. Letty would have quite a lot to tell her husband when they were alone together.

'There's one difficulty,' said Mrs. Batt. 'Mr. Dommett was a vegetarian . . .'

If Dommett had been a cannibal she couldn't have pronounced it more dramatically. And, as though this idiosyncrasy had touched a tender cord, she shed a few tears. This she did without any facial movement, like those dolls that weep under diaphragmatic pressure.

'He used to say that vegetarian diet was a way to long

life . . . And now after all his trouble, he's been cut off in his prime.'

Which was an affectionate overstatement, as Dommett must have been nearer 80 than 70.

'He insisted on me being the same, as he used to say he wished me to have a long life too.'

'Have you any eggs . . .?'

Mrs. Batt confessed that although Mr. Dommett regarded eggs with disfavour she had kept a few in hiding.

'I was always partial to an egg and sometimes after all that vegetarian food, I'd get longing so much that I couldn't sleep or, if I did get to sleep, I'd dream about eggs . . . poached, boiled, scrambled, omelettes . . . So, I kept a few and when he was out I'd poach myself one or two on toast . . . or else I'd get up in the night . . . Nothing wrong in that, was there?'

'Of course not. Where are they now?'

Mrs. Batt disappeared through an adjacent door and, without disclosing her hiding-place, returned with a basin containing a dozen eggs. A short time later she and Mrs. Littlejohn laid the kitchen table and invited the men to a meal of omelettes and cheese. Mrs. Batt said that Mr. Dommett had been fond of cheese and had eaten considerable quantities of it. There was a large Stilton half consumed to prove this. She said she didn't like cheese. It didn't agree with her. Chief Superintendent Winstanley excused himself from joining the tea party. He had several routine matters to attend to in connection with the crime but would return later.

At first the conversation was stilted and formal, but it

became easier after the ladies had finished serving and joined in the feast. Naturally, the talk was funereal until Littlejohn changed the subject and gently moved it in the direction that suited the police. Sadd, who had been invited to the meal, concentrated on his food. He was a meat lover and had never even seen an omelette before.

' When did you last see Mr. Dommett, Mrs. Batt?'

' At ten o'clock this morning. I gave him his coffee, if such you could call it. It was made with dandelions. And then I went off to Aylesdon to do my weekly shopping. The shops won't deliver out here, there being nobody but us to serve, except when the week-enders in the village arrive for a short stay. Mr. Dommett sold his car a long time ago and now I have to telephone to Aylesdon for a taxi. Mr. Dommett had calculated which way was cheapest before he sold the car.'

' Was Mr. Dommett in his usual frame of mind? I mean did he seem any different from usual.'

' No. He was just the same. He never talked much. He was always nervous about the property and on the look out for intruders. Especially now that we're on our own. When Mr. Bugler and Mr. Waddilove were here they used to be on the look out, too.'

' How long have they been gone? I used to know them years ago and I'm surprised to hear they were still with Mr. Dommett. I thought they were part of the coroner's staff . . .'

' Well, whatever they were, he kept them on after he retired.'

' What did they find to do with their time?'

Mrs. Batt indicated the room around her with a wide sweep of the hand.

'They built this place . . . The whole of the property had been empty for years and the stables . . . This was part of them . . . The stables were all tumbledown and dirty. When Mr. Dommett retired . . .'

'That must be eight years ago?'

'Seven years last October. When he retired he decided to come and live here. His wife was alive then and I was their housekeeper when they were living at Slingsby Magna. This property came to Mrs. Dommett in a will and was a real liability. A proper white elephant. Nobody wanted it and it wasn't fit to live in. But I think Mr. Dommett had an idea of occupying a part of it from the very start. He talked of making the manor house into flats, but that was a mad idea. He couldn't hope to attract buyers for flats when the village itself had been deserted by people who found it too remote and spooky. Mrs. Dommett wasn't well and I think on that account mainly Mr. Dommett decided just to make the stables into a home and abandon his scheme about the rest.'

'But why come here at all? Did he sell his place at Slingsby Magna?'

'Yes. Slingsby was a growing locality with building estates and such like and Mr. Dommett said he wanted to be where it was quiet and out of the way . . .'

Mrs. Batt lowered her voice and spoke as if to herself.

'He'd something on his mind. I sometimes thought he was afraid of something and wanted to get out of the way of it.'

'What made you think that?'

'Well . . . He was always on the look out. He'd a loaded shotgun up in his bedroom and a revolver in a drawer of his dressing table. Why should he want those? He couldn't shoot at the boys who came on motor bikes with his guns. And why did he keep on Mr. Bugler and Mr. Waddilove if not to act as his guards as they'd done when he was county coroner? Why spend all that money on their wages? The work they did on the property didn't pay for that.'

Mrs. Batt, once wound up, went on and on, posing questions and not pausing for answers.

'More cheese, Mr. Sadd?' said Mrs. Littlejohn, interrupting to give them a breathing space.

Sadd was a man of great appetite and when he arrived home after his daily toil his wife fed him with gigantic meals. 'Always remember, the way to a man's heart is through his stomach, Miriam,' her mother had taught her and she had profited thereby. Sadd had disposed of his omelette in a few short gulps and, had his manners permitted it, would have done the same with the cheese, which after a preliminary meagre helping he continued to regard wistfully.

Mrs. Batt poured out her story, non-stop. With only the laconic Mr. Dommett for company after the departure of Bugler and Waddilove, Mrs. Batt, naturally garrulous, had had to resort to talking to herself. Now she avidly seized the opportunity to unburden herself.

'Mr. Bugler was a gentleman, but I never fancied Waddilove. To start with, his name sounded made up. Who ever heard of a Waddilove before? It didn't sound decent, did it? As though his name was Waddy and you were being a bit forward calling him " Love " . . .'

' What happened to them, Mrs. Batt?'

' Mr. Waddilove had a heart attack one morning. Sudden it was. He was dead before we could get the doctor to him.'

' When was that?'

' About two months ago. Mr. Dommett was very upset. Not so much about him dying, but because he was left here on his own. Also, he'd had a row with Waddilove and, in my opinion, it caused him to have his attack.'

' What was it all about?'

' Waddilove had been drinking. Mr. Dommett kept two or three bottles of whisky . . . Medicinal, it was, and Waddilove had drunk the lot. Mr. Dommett found the empty bottles in the dustbin . . .'

' Mr. Dommett still had Bugler, hadn't he?'

' He gave in his resignation the day after Mr. Waddilove died. Mr. Dommett took that bad, too. There was another row then. They shouted terribly at one another. Mr. Bugler told Mr. Dommett he'd as good as killed Mr. Waddilove and told Mr. Dommett to his face that he'd drunk some of the whisky himself and what was he going to do about it. He said he wouldn't stay on in this tumble-down hole. That's what he called it.'

Her eyes grew wide and wild and her breast heaved as though she were joining in the fray.

' What kind of a man was Bugler?'

' He was an educated man, was Mr. B. He used big words, too. He said Mr. Waddilove had *sustained* him. In the row, he gave as much as he got and he packed up and went after the funeral.'

' Where did that take place?'

' He didn't seem to have any family that we could find, and Mr. Bugler said he hadn't. So he was buried at Cold Barsby. Mr. Dommett didn't even go to the funeral. He didn't believe in God . . . So I wonder what's happening to him now that he's passed on.'

Tears squirted from her eyes again, and to hide her emotion she took and ate a large piece of cheese before she realised what she was doing.

' Where did Bugler go?'

' He gave me his address before he went, so I could send on any letters that came for him. Not that he got many. One, now and then, from Australia, where he'd got relatives, that's all. We always got on well together. He used to tease me now and then. He called me Lucy, too. I didn't, of course, go so far as to call him Reginald. I just called him Mr. B.'

She paused and preened herself. She seemed to ' fancy ' Bugler and her chief regret was that he had gone.

' Will you give me his address?'

She had memorised it and didn't even need to look it up.

' 44, Tasman Road, Wimbledon, Surrey. He's gone to stay with his sister who is the widow of a butler who'd been in service in London at a house where she'd been parlour-maid. Mr. B. went to stay temporarily with his sister although he once told me they didn't get on well together. He must have changed his mind since then.'

Littlejohn paused to finish his meal. Mrs. Batt was a mine

of information and showed no reticence in dispensing it. He wished he'd asked Sadd to take notes. But Sadd was still busy with the cheese.

By the time the meal was finished evening was falling. The atmosphere surrounding the sad ruin of the manor with its barren trees and desolate garden, grew eerie. Winstanley had sent more policemen to guard the place and they could be seen forcing their ways through the brambles and warning off intruders. The news must have spread to neighbouring villages and although the population of the locality was thin, a small crowd of people had gathered at the main gate and some even intruded in the spinney where the body had been found, and had to be ordered away. There was a thin line of cars on the road, too, as though the ill-tidings had spread farther afield and stimulated their owners to make a grisly outing of the affair. They seemed filled with savage curiosity and resented being kept at bay by the police who urged them to go home.

' What has happened to the dog?'

Littlejohn had forgotten the animal and seeing the trespassers in the distance wondered why it was not on its usual patrol.

' Grimes must have taken him home with him. It's really Grimes's dog and follows him about,' said Mrs Batt who was clearing away the dishes.

Sadd had gone to join his fellow constables and now there were only the Littlejohns left to keep the housekeeper company.

' Grimes? Is that the gardener?'

Mrs. Batt made a snorting noise.

'You can call him the gardener if you like. He never does any gardening. He was here when Mr. Dommett and his wife first arrived. He goes with the place, a part of the manor, so to speak. He's deaf and a bit short in his wits.'

'What were his duties?'

'Mainly hanging about. He doesn't get much pay. He occupies a cottage between here and the village. The cottage belongs to the manor house and Grimes was in it when Mr. Dommett took over. He didn't disturb him. I guess he was another man to guard the place.'

'You keep talking about guarding the place. What is there to guard?'

Mrs. Batt gave him a peculiar sideways look.

'Gipsies. There's a lot of them around and they're always hanging about wanting to pitch their caravans here. And there are the young hooligans on motor-bikes. They come from the towns and ride into the village as if they own it, breaking into the houses and picking up what they can get. The place needs some men about it to keep off the intruders.'

Men about the place. Littlejohn wondered if Sebastian Dommett had had in mind recruiting *him* as a member of his security army.

'It was you who answered my telephone call this morning, Mrs. Batt?'

'Yes. Mr. Dommett said he'd written to you and you would be calling to see him.'

'Why did he want to see me?'

'He never told me, but I got the idea that he thought you

might care to come and live here, with Mr. B. and Waddilove having gone and there being only Grimes left. He was
considering making another house like this one out of
number two stables, next to these. If that was what he was
thinking of doing, I'm sure it wouldn't have suited you and
your wife. A high officer of the police like yourself, sir,
wouldn't be wanting to act as security guard, especially in
a queer ruin like this. I don't know what he was thinking
of making such a suggestion.'

'Nor do I. He was a strange man, though, and had
despised the police ever since his daughter married a constable. Where is she, by the way?'

'The last I heard of them they were in Canada. Mr.
Dommett never forgave them. She used to send him a card
every Christmas, but he never got in contact with her as
far as I know.'

Mrs. Batt and Mrs. Littlejohn did the washing up and
talked of cooking and other matters of domestic economy.
Mrs. Batt seemed relieved when Sadd returned from his
wandering.

'Oh, there you are, Mr. Sadd. I'm glad to see you. It's
time we were off to my sister's. I'm not staying here on my
own. It's haunted. More so now, with Mr. Dommett having
got himself murdered. He'll come back and haunt the
place along with the rest of the spooks. He always looked
like one who would haunt after he died. He didn't believe
in God, you know . . .'

'A lot of rubbish,' said Sadd, who had grown morose at
the thought of taking Mrs. Batt to her sister's instead of
returning home to one of his wife's prodigious meals.

'Besides, one of our constables is staying here all night. You'd be quite safe . . .'

Instead of replying, Mrs. Batt left them and they could hear her footsteps upstairs and then bumping noises as though she were tearing up the floor. Then more bumpings down the stairs and she appeared dragging a very large suitcase, and clad in a green coat and black hat.

She panted from her efforts and then addressed Sadd.

'I *will not* stop here another night. So you can put my bag in your car and let's be off. It's growing dark . . .'

She paused as if an awful thought had struck her.

'Where's Mr. Dommett?'

'In the mortuary . . .'

'Will there have to be an inquest?'

'There's always an inquest when there's been a murder.'

'Will I be there?'

'I guess so . . .'

'But I didn't do it . . .'

'I thought you wanted to get to your sister's. Come on and let's be off.'

Mrs. Batt suddenly grew excited at the prospect of visiting her sister and shook hands all round, including Sadd.

'What's that for?' he said, 'I'm going with you.'

'I'll come back one day for the rest of my things. My brother-in-law, Herbert, has a car and will bring me. They'll let me in, won't they?'

And she and Sadd departed, still arguing and asking questions of each other. As the car left they seemed to be quarrelling about the route they would take.

Then Littlejohn and Letty were left alone in that eerie place with dusk falling.

'I wish we were home, Tom,' she said. 'Home among familiar things. This place seems out of another world, a bit frightening.'

'Winstanley should be here very soon and then we'll go. It's a wonder Mrs. Batt stayed on after the two men had gone. Can you imagine her and Dommett alone in this place, night after night? Dommett afraid of something or someone and prowling about with a gun. And Mrs. Batt, sure the place was haunted and scared out of her wits.'

'We haven't seen the rest of the house, have we?'

'Do you want to explore it?'

'Not just now. I feel like Mrs. Batt must have been. Scared.'

Then there was a diversion outside. In the half light they could see Grimes shambling across the courtyard with his dog at his heels. The animal must have scented intruders and it charged in the direction of the constables still guarding the spinney. There was a great commotion among the thickets as the animal arrived there and Grimes, unable to hear it but aware that something was happening, stuck two fingers in his mouth and whistled shrilly. Almost at once the dog emerged again and bounded back to him. He kicked it and it whimpered and slunk to his heel.

Winstanley appeared and they could see him rebuking Grimes, who didn't hear a word and nodded and grinned as though the conversation pleased him. Then Grimes turned on his heel and went off in the direction from which he had come, presumably making for home.

'Are you two here all on your own?' said Winstanley as he entered the room.

'Yes. Sadd has gone off with Mrs. Batt, who's staying the night with her sister. She refuses to sleep here alone.'

Winstanley made himself comfortable in one of the chairs in front of the dead fire and stretched his legs.

'I'm sorry to have left you in charge of the place while we attended to the formalities, Tom. This is going to be a strange case. Who would want to kill Dommett? I grant you a coroner has to contend with some funny affairs, even murder cases, but I can't think that, on that account any-one would want to murder him for attending to his business. What do you think?'

'There's more to it than that, Frank. Mrs. Batt tells me that Dommett was afraid of something or someone and given to prowling about his property armed with a gun. Until a short time ago he had two guards here with him, men who formerly accompanied him on his rounds as coroner. He was attacked once on a case and after that never seemed to move without them. One of them, Waddi-love, died recently of a heart attack after a row with Dommett and, arising from it, the other bodyguard, Bugler, also had a slanging match with Dommett, packed his bag and cleared off. He's now living with his sister in London. Dommett and Mrs. Batt were left on their own here. Can you imagine the pair of them isolated in this ruin? Mrs. Batt says the place is haunted. No wonder she's concocted a ghost.'

'They had Grimes with them, too. He's enough to scare the wits out of anybody, prowling about the ruins. I just

met him and told him to keep away from this place and
confine himself to his cottage and that locality. And he's
not as deaf as he makes out, according to the constable who
shares this patch with Sadd. A chap called Plover, who's
lived in this locality all his life. He says Grimes is a half-
wit, said to be the illegitimate son of somebody who once
lived in this district all his life. He says Grimes is a half-
annuity when he died. In the circumstances, Grimes might
be a suspect. He might have resented Dommett's intrusion
here or else Dommett might have offended him and he got
violent . . .'

'Did anything turn up during the search of the spot
where we found Dommett?'

'Not a thing. Did you ever hear about Dommett's
background, Tom?'

'I know he was a county coroner and I encountered him
now and then when Scotland Yard used to give a hand to
provincial police before they had their own expert C.I.D.s.
He was an awkward customer and very rude in the course
of his inquiries. His daughter ran away with a constable and
that seemed to make him hate the police ever after. I
wonder if they ever became reconciled. According to Mrs.
Batt, she and her husband went to Canada and she kept in
touch with her father although he didn't reciprocate. I
guess she'll have to be told about his death.'

Winstanley looked across at Mrs. Littlejohn.

'Are you feeling cold, Mrs. Littlejohn?'

'Yes. This place is cold without a fire at this time of day.
Besides, as Mrs. Batt says, it's spooky and depressing. I
think it's time we made our way home; I've had enough of

Mr. Sebastian Dommett for one day. I know a policeman's wife shouldn't interfere in his duties, but there are limits and this is one of them.'

' Just let me tell you some more about Dommett and then we'll go. We have a file about Dommett at headquarters. We've had several encounters with him. Twice he's taken pot shots at trespassers on his property. We couldn't have that sort of thing, even if he *had* been a county coroner. The gun wasn't licensed either and he had a revolver without a permit, too, and brandished it a time or two at intruders. We granted him a permit, in view of the remoteness of this place, but he promised to behave himself properly. Every time we dealt with his affairs there was an awful row. He was so arrogant.'

He rose and prepared to go.

' There's one other thing, too. Before he became a coroner, Dommett was in practice in London with another lawyer called Gutteridge. Dommett and Gutteridge. Gutteridge embezzled quite a large amount and absconded. They caught him hiding somewhere in Scotland. He died in gaol. That affair, of course, broke up the partnership and ruined the good name of the partners. Dommett, who was a very competent lawyer, got a coroner's job and I guess the disaster, combined with his daughter's escapade, made him bitter. I would say it made him slightly mad. However, it makes one very interested in his past. There may be something there which has been the cause of the present tragedy.'

With that, they left the place and locked up. Night had fallen and an owl was hooting in one of the trees in the garden of the ruined house.

'What a set-up,' said Winstanley. 'Night after night here with Dommett scared of something nobody else knew anything about. This place has a bad reputation. The family was on the king's side during the Civil War and the squire put up some resistance when Cromwell's men turned up. They slaughtered the squire and his two sons and set fire to the place. It was rebuilt later and the last owner of the inhabited manor hanged himself in the hall . . .'

The recital was interrupted by the sudden appearance of a dark figure at the broken gate. He shone his torch at the three of them.

'Beg pardon, sirs. I didn't know it was you . . .'

'We're just leaving it to you, Plover. When is your relief due?'

'In half-an-hour, sir,' said P.C. Plover, 'And I'll be glad to see him. This place gives you the creeps, if I may say so.'

They couldn't see much of him, except a large nose and two sad eyes under his flat cap.

'You'd better take the key and make yourself comfortable in Dommett's house, Plover.'

'I'd rather be out of doors, sir, if it's all the same to you. The place is haunted, they say, sir. I've always said I don't believe such old women's talk and have never experienced it before. But after what's happened today, I don't know, sir . . . I just don't know.'

P.C. Plover accompanied them to the main gate, where they left him to his lonely vigil.

4

Mr. Bugler at Home

FORTIFIED BY the permission of his superiors, Winstanley asked Littlejohn if one of Scotland Yard's officers could call on Bugler at Wimbledon and make preliminary inquiries about his association with Sebastian Dommett. Having known him in days gone by, Littlejohn was curious about how Bugler had developed, and offered to call on him instead. In the days of his active labours as coroner Dommett had never travelled anywhere without his strange bodyguard, Bugler and Waddilove. They were known by the police in the area served by Dommett as Tweedledum and Tweedledee. Only behind their backs, of course. Once when Dommett heard them called by their nicknames, there had been a terrible hullabaloo, for he had no sense of humour whatever. He had even talked about contempt of court! Littlejohn had forgotten which was which of them and wondered who would greet him when he called on him in Wimbledon.

44, Tasman Road was a terraced house in the middle of a row of similar properties in what might be described as the working-class part of the town. Iron railings separated what had once been a garden from the pavement and a flagged path led to the front door. The front garden had been completely covered by a surface of concrete by the late Mr. Flowerdew, Bugler's brother-in-law, who had retired there on his ill-gotten gains, after receiving the sack from his post as butler in Paddington for receiving substantial commissions from the tradesmen. Mr. Flowerdew had no intention of soiling his hands by digging and raising flowers.

Littlejohn beat on the knocker and, after eyeing him up and down through a chink in the front window curtains, Mrs. Flowerdew opened the door. She was a prim little woman who must have been good looking in her prime, but now, in her sixties, with her hair cut short and a pair of fancy spectacles in green frames on her nose, she looked worried and pale and ill-tempered. Her gas bill was overdue and she thought at first that Littlejohn had arrived from the gas company to threaten her.

'Is Mr. Bugler at home?'

Her lips tightened as though she was wondering what Reginald had been up to.

'Wait a minute. Who shall I say wants him?'

Littlejohn introduced himself. There was a silence as though Mrs. Flowerdew was considering her next move. Then she left Littlejohn at the open door and vanished down the narrow corridor into the back room.

'Come in,' she said when she returned and he followed her through the semi-darkness to the inner room. A smell of stewed beef and onions permeated the place, as though lunch was being vigorously prepared.

'Chief Superintendent Littlejohn,' she announced with a trace of her old manner as parlourmaid.

A little fat man with a bald head and flushed cheeks rose from the armchair by the gas stove. He had been reading his morning paper and a glass and a bottle of whisky were on the table at his elbow. The grin on his face and the rotating motion of his body as he rose indicated that he was probably half drunk already.

'Well, this is a pleasure,' he said and extended a flabby hand. 'What brings you here, Mr. Littlejohn?'

The room was stuffy and was probably what Bugler regarded as a cosy retreat. There was an old suite of furniture with antimacassars on the backs of easy chairs. The window overlooked the rear of similar houses in a parallel street, with a view over a long narrow yard, which might once have been a garden and which had been skimmed over with concrete like the one at the front. Beside a ramshackle shed was a pile of orange boxes, the latter partly chopped up for firelighters.

Bugler invited Littlejohn to take a seat and bounced into his own chair again. Littlejohn wished he had remained standing, for the interior of the armchair was full of loose springs and he could not find a comfortable spot. The walls of the room were ornamented with photographs of groups of men, presumably at conferences or cricket matches and over the fireplace in the place of honour was a portrait of a man who strongly resembled Bugler and was wearing an academic cap and gown, leaning against a piano, one hand clutching his diploma and with the other he was caressing the keys.

'My father,' said Bugler briefly, as he observed Littlejohn wondering who the man might be.

Bugler offered him a drink and looked surprised when Littlejohn excused himself.

'I forgot. You're on duty, sir. What's it all about?'

'I've called to tell you that Mr. Dommett died yesterday. He was murdered.'

Mr. Bugler paused to allow the information to sink in.

'Murdered? Surely not.'

'Yes. We found him dead in the spinney near the main drive of the manor house.'

Bugler turned pale and poured himself a stiff drink and downed it in three swift gulps. His manner changed from cordiality to caution.

'I hope you don't think I had anything to do with it. I left Mr. Dommett's employ several weeks ago and I haven't seen him or been near the place since.'

'I'm not suggesting you are involved in the crime at all. I've called to ask if you can give us information which might help us in our inquiries. Mr. Dommett was a strange man and had strange ways . . .'

'Nobody knows that better than me. I worked with him for more than 40 years and I tolerated his eccentricities all that time. Finally, I just couldn't stand it any more and I gave him notice. Things you put up with when you're young become unendurable when you get older . . .'

At which sage remark he drank some more whisky.

'How did you first meet Mr. Dommett?'

Bugler frowned and pursed his lips. He was wearing carpet slippers and kept sliding his heels in and out of them. Finally, he got on his feet and began to pace the room.

'I answered an advertisement in the newspaper for a clerk in the office of Dommett and Gutteridge, solicitors in London. Over 20 years I rose in the office till I became their managing clerk until the firm was dissolved.'

He paused to collect his thoughts.

'You might say I ran the firm on the conveyancing side. It's a pity I wasn't in charge of the accounts, as well. They might have avoided the crash.'

'What happened?'

'Mr. Gutteridge turned out to be a wrong 'un. He had been falsifying the books and appropriating the moneys of certain wealthy clients. He made a run for it after being found out, but the police caught up with him before he could get out of the country. He got ten years for it and died in prison. The mystery was, what did he do with the money? It was nearly £40,000. Defalcations of that sort were covered by insurance, otherwise Mr. Dommett would have had to pay up. The insurance company made a complete investigation of where the funds had gone but they couldn't find a trace of it. And Mr. Gutteridge wouldn't co-operate in finding it.'

'How long had it been going on?'

'Over ten years. The firm was a very old one and Gutteridge's father and grandfather had been members of it. They had a lot of large trusts to handle, many of them very old ones, and Mr. Gutteridge had charge of them. He did it very craftily and carefully, but, in the end, he got too deep in his frauds and had to sell securities belonging to some of the trusts and he forged the transfers.'

'How was he found out?'

'Bad luck. You see, if you're running a fraud of that sort, you must keep a cool head and also maintain control of the books you're falsifying. And if you sell a trust's shares and pocket the money, you must remember that the dividends on such shares are paid to beneficiaries under the trust and you must keep paying the money to them out of your own pocket. Otherwise they'd be inquiring why they hadn't received their usual payments. In all the years he was working the fraud Mr. Gutteridge never went on holidays. He never missed a day at the office and personally kept the keys of his private safe. Naturally, nobody thought he was defrauding the firm. And with the trusts being always handled by his family before him, nobody, not even Mr. Dommett, would have interfered. And then, after all his trouble, his bad luck came. He was knocked down by a bicycle in the street and taken unconscious to the hospital. His skull was fractured. Not badly, but enough to keep him in bed for a fortnight. When he recovered consciousness, he talked right away of getting up and going back to the office, but they wouldn't let him . . .'

'And his fraud was discovered . . . by whom?'

'Mr. Dommett! Somebody inquired about one of the trusts and Mr. Dommett insisted on taking the keys from Gutteridge and he opened the safe to look at the books. You knew Mr. Dommett in the old days, sir. He was very smart. There wasn't much got past him. He had the books in his office for days together, checked them, worked at night, and by the time Gutteridge was discharged from hospital the case against him was complete. I never knew what was said to Gutteridge while he was at home convalescent and when he returned to the office. I know Mr. Gutteridge pleaded with Mr. Dommett on bended knees to give him time to try to put things right. But Dommett wouldn't hear of it. He called in the police. The accountants were sent for and Gutteridge was arrested, tried and sentenced. Ten years. It was a terrible time for all of us. And the firm's reputation suffered. Mr. Dommett packed up and took on the coroner's job. After all, he'd earned professional credit by divulging the fraud at once and helping all he could to put matters right. He'd no difficulty in getting the appointment. It left me out of a job and he offered me the post of coroner's officer and I took it.'

'Where did Waddilove come in? He used to accompany you on inquests, too, didn't he?'

'Yes. He was one of the messengers at the coroner's court. Mr. Dommett took him on as a sort of assistant to me. Not long after Gutteridge was imprisoned Gutteridge's son assaulted Mr. Dommett. He said he held Mr. Dommett responsible for his father's downfall and he waited till Mr. Dommett was alone at an inquest somewhere in the county and attacked him. He beat him up good and proper and Mr. Dommett was in hospital for a fortnight. After that, he was scared of another attack. As a matter of fact, I think it turned his head a bit. He never went out alone on an inquiry after it. I shouldn't say it of the dead, but Mr. Dommett, although a bully, was a coward.'

'What qualification had Waddilove for the job?'

'He'd been in the army before he got the place at court. And he'd held one of the army boxing championships. Mr Dommett was never attacked again, but if he had been

Waddilove would have given a good account of himself . . .'

Bugler lowered his voice and said reverently.

'Poor Waddilove died shortly before I left Mr. Dommett's place.'

Probably stimulated by the whisky he had consumed, his eyes bulged and filled with tears and looked ready to leave their sockets and swim down his cheeks.

'The poor chap was bored to death by that place, took too much drink and had a heart attack. It was like losing my right arm, sir, when poor Harold passed on. He was a good pal . . .'

And, carried away by his own eloquence, Mr. Bugler burst into tears.

'Excuse me, Mr. Littlejohn. But when you've worked with a man for as long as Waddy and me were together it's a bit of a wrench when you have to part.'

Bugler dried his tears and blew his nose.

The interview was briefly interrupted by Bugler's sister who, without a word, opened the door of the room and quickly closed it again with a bang. A blast of onions blew across the room.

'That means lunch is ready, sir, so we mustn't be long. I'm sorry I can't invite you to have a bite with us at our humble table, but we weren't prepared for company, you see . . .'

'Don't worry. I must be off. But first tell me why Dommett went to live in such a forsaken place.'

Bugler lowered his voice and spoke ominously.

'He was afraid of something. The way he acted, with burglar alarms in the house, shotguns about and a revolver, prowling round the grounds keeping me and Waddy on his payroll. He must have been afraid . . .'

'What was he afraid of?'

'Don't ask me. He never took me into his confidence. We was his bodyguard, not his confessors.'

And, as though pleased with his choice of words, Bugler repeated them.

'. . . Wasn't his confessors.'

'Do you think young Gutteridge was the cause of it all. Did Dommett think he was on his trail for another beating-up?'

'Young Tim Gutteridge is dead. Motor smash. So it wasn't him the boss was afraid of.'

'Gutteridge had another son, hadn't he?'

'Yes. He'd just qualified as a doctor when his father went to prison. He emigrated to Canada and we lost touch with him. I don't know where he is now.'

'Had Dommett any enemies?'

'Not who'd want to go to the extent of murdering him. As you doubtless know from your past dealings with the boss, he had no friends. Kept himself to himself and sooner or later insulted those who wished to be friendly. He was a bitter, domineering man, as you remember from your encounters with him in the witness-box. He was particularly hostile to the police.'

'His daughter had eloped with a policeman, hadn't she?'

Littlejohn smiled at the recollection of the affair, but Bugler didn't see any fun in it.

'He was like a madman about it. Never forgave her. She

tried a time or two to get reconciled, but Mr. Dommett would not have it. Cut her off completely.'

'What happened to her and her husband? Do you know?'

'They emigrated to Canada and he got a good job there in the police. He was shot in a bank raid and she was left a widow for a time. She was a beauty and wouldn't have much trouble in getting another husband, which she did. She wrote to tell her father and the news nearly killed him. He got in such a rage that he had a slight heart attack. As well he might. Do you know who she married?'

Littlejohn could guess, but he left to Bugler the pleasure of telling him.

'Who was it?'

'Dr. Chris Gutteridge.'

'I thought you said you didn't know where the doctor ended up.'

'I don't. He was in Toronto when he married Imogen Dommett. The last time she wrote to her father they were in Montreal. I guess you could find out from the Canadian medical directory. You'll have to let her know about her father's death, won't you?'

'How did you get to know all this? You said you weren't in Dommett's confidence. Did he tell you?'

'No. It was Waddy who found out. Waddy used to read her letters to her father. He had a great thirst for information, had Waddy, poor chap. He used to read all the incoming correspondence. Sometimes when he hadn't much to do, he got bored and went on the prowl. He had a key that fitted Mr. Dommett's desk and used to look in it now and then when the boss was not about. He said he'd a right to do so, just to find out what the future held in store for us. He'd a great sense of humour. Although it wasn't much trouble getting hold of Miss Imogen's letters. The boss tore them up in a rage and chucked them in the wastepaper basket. Waddy used to reassemble them and read them that way. It's a pity he's dead. He was a mine of information and would have been very useful to you.'

'But he must have passed on all the news to you, didn't he?'

'Not all of it. He must have gathered quite a lot of stuff that he never mentioned to me. He used to tell me what you might call the sensational or juicy bits, but he kept a lot to himself, I'm sure.'

'What were the sensational and juicy bits, as you call them, Mr. Bugler? Do you remember?'

Mr. Bugler rubbed his chin as though it stimulated his memory.

'There were several letters from Imogen in most affectionate terms. The boss tore them up and threw them away. It always seemed to me that somebody kept an eye on Dommett's movements and let Imogen know about them. It may have been her mother during her lifetime. She knew when he moved to the manor house and took up his residence in the stables. And it wasn't the boss who informed her, because he never wrote to her. He cut himself off from the rest of the world and in consequence received little or no correspondence. Sometimes there wouldn't be anything through the post for weeks at a time.'

'And then what sort of communications did he receive?'

' Now and then a letter from the bank . . .'

' Where did he bank?'

' Garfitts Bank. They have a sub-branch at Ashby Newbold, and he used them. I guess he didn't want to deal with a busy place.'

' What was the bank writing about?'

' Routine mostly. He cashed cheques through the post unless any of us was going to Ashby, which wasn't often. Waddy kept an eye on the incoming mail, but now and then a letter would arrive that Mr. Dommett locked in the safe. There is a small safe in the cupboard to the right of the fireplace in the dining room. Waddy hadn't a key for that. It used to make him mad when he couldn't keep in touch, as he called it. And then there was the post-cards . . .'

' What about them?'

' A practical joke, I think. The first one arrived about three years ago. And one started to arrive about every six months. It infuriated Mr. Dommett. You see, somebody had got his address. There were no threats in them. Just silly messages.'

' Such as . . .?'

' There was a view of Scarborough. The message, as far as I can remember, was something like " Greetings from Scarborough. Hope you are well. See you one of these days, you old bastard." There was no signature or initials. The postman handed it to Mrs. Batt who brought it in. After that, more cards arrived now and then, but we were never able to read them, because the boss told the postman not to hand over anything through the post, but to put it in the post-box of which Mr. Dommett had the only key. He tore them all up and burned them, but we knew they'd arrived, more or less, by the traces of them in the grate or wastepaper basket. When there wasn't a fire in the grate he used to set fire to them with a match and crumble up the ashes. At other times, we knew when one had arrived because he seemed more scared than ever and increased the precautions and told us to be more alert, as people were trespassing. One that wasn't properly burned was sent from Ilfracombe, but the message had been destroyed.'

'Had Waddilove any relatives or connections living?'

'One brother. He'd been in the army and when he retired from the service he took up a job as bank messenger.'

'Which bank?'

'Merganser's, in Fenchurch Street. He retired from there. We tried to contact him when Waddy died but he'd left his last known address in rooms in Croydon. Mr. Dommett told us to let it drop. He didn't want strangers visiting us.'

Bugler's sister re-appeared looking very harassed.

'Your dinner's getting cold,' she said with a toss of her head, and catching Littlejohn's eye she gave him a little curtsey, as she'd done as parlourmaid in the golden years of her life, and departed.

Bugler conducted Littlejohn to the door. On the doorstep before he left him Littlejohn stopped to ask another question.

'What about Mrs. Batt? What were the relations between her and Sebastian Dommett?'

'They got on well together. With anybody but Mr. Dommett, I'd say they was very intimate, but there was nothing of that sort. All the same, they was as thick as thieves and she seemed to be the only real friend he'd got.'

' I may call on you again, Mr. Bugler. Thanks for your help . . . Oh, by the way, where were you all yesterday?'

Bugler slowly turned his head and glared at Littlejohn.

' I hope you don't think I had anything to do with poor Mr. Dommett's death . . .'

' Not at all. Mere routine. We've got to know.'

' I see. Well, I was at home all day from the time I got up at 8.30, till I went to bed at 11.00, except for about quarter of an hour, when I walked round the block and got my morning paper. I collect foreign stamps and was sorting them out and listening to the telly. My sister will confirm all I say . . .'

The coalman thereupon arrived and as the position of the cellar necessitated the humping of the bags through the front door the meeting broke up.

Mr. Wilberforce Waddilove

WILLY, (short for Wilberforce), Waddilove was found with
unusual ease. When he returned to Scotland Yard after
lunch, Littlejohn rang up the War Office, whence, as an
ex-regular, Willy received a pension. The district police had
done the rest. Willy was at present living at Mrs. Cuffright's
boarding-house – grandiosely described as the Waldstein
Hotel – in Great Duke Street, Paddington. He was night
watchman at a fur store in Bond Street, watching by night
and sleeping most of the following morning.

The Waldstein was scheduled for demolition and replace-
ment by a multi-storeyed block of flats. At one time it had
been an elegant Georgian town house with a pillared
entrance and a graceful staircase sailing aloft. Even in the
early days of Mrs. Cuffright's management the place had
been a select establishment, but the late Cuffright had taken
to drink and left his wife with more than she could handle.
Now, it was seedy and forlorn and Mrs. Cuffright was a
bag of nerves, worried that any time now the order would
be served to turn her into the street. She met Littlejohn
at the door, thought he had come about the eviction
and recoiled into the dim interior without even asking
the nature of his visit. Littlejohn followed her in. Where-

at she shut the front door and stood with her back to it.

' What do you want?'

Littlejohn handed her his card. This gave her no relief.

' The police! Has he actually put the matter in your hands? I will pay his bill at the end of the month when my residents pay theirs . . .'

More explanations and Mrs. Cuffright recovered somewhat and told Littlejohn that Mr. Waddilove occupied a room on the top floor.

' I regret we have no lift. The building was never constructed for such amenities,' she said in the affected voice she had used when the Walpole was in its heyday.

Littlejohn toiled up the stairs to what had once been the servants' quarters. At the first floor, the shabby carpet ceased and a strip of linoleum took its place. There were two more floors and then the three small rooms under the attics. Littlejohn knocked on the first door he came to. There was a dead silence. Instinctively, Littlejohn felt there was someone there. Then a whisper. He knocked again. A woman's voice answered.

' Who is it?'

' Police.'

More whispering.

' What do you want?'

It was a man's voice this time.

' Is that Mr. Waddilove?'

' I said what do you want?'

' I want your help in connection with a recent murder. You can either open up and answer my questions here, or I'll send a constable to bring you to the police station.'

'Who's been murdered? I've had nothing to do with any murder, so why pick on me?'

'Are you going to open the door . . .?'

'Wait a minute then . . .'

There was more whispering in the room and the occupants seemed to be quarrelling *sotto voce*.

Suddenly, the door flew open and a buxom scantily-clad woman, her crossed arms protecting her copious breasts, skipped out, crossed the landing and vanished into the room opposite, banging the door. Her bare feet seemed hardly to touch the ground and it was all over before Littlejohn had time to properly take it in.

'Who's that?' said Littlejohn to the man who had thrown out the luscious fugitive.

'Never you mind. She's a friend of mine and has nothing to do with the police or murders or any other sort of crime. She comes in now and then to help me with the housework.'

'I can see that,' said Littlejohn.

Willy Waddilove had been in the regular army but had lost all traces of it. He held himself with a hunched back and his arms dangling like a monkey. Had he pulled himself together he would have been tall. He was flabby, thick-lipped and red faced and his hair was grey and tousled. He was in his stockinged feet and wore a soiled open-necked shirt and trousers with his braces hanging loose. Littlejohn had caught him at an awkward time, but Willy didn't seem to mind. He tried to recover his dignity, but didn't succeed.

'What's all this about murder and why am I being

pestered by the police? I don't know anything about a murder.'

'Did you know your brother was dead?'

'Which one? There were five of us. I thought they were all dead. I was notified when three of them died. I thought the fourth had died and nobody had bothered to inform me. Was it Harold?'

'Yes. He died a few weeks ago.'

'Was he murdered? I didn't do it, and I shan't go in mourning for him in any case. He never bothered about me. Why should I worry about him?'

He paused as a thought struck him.

'Did he leave any money?'

'We don't know anything about his personal affairs. He died a natural death at Swinton in Midshire.'

'I don't know anything about it. Harold and I didn't get on well. Never did. He was older than me and used to chuck his weight about. I wasn't interested in him or what he did. We haven't met for years. There was always a row when we met. Was he still working for old Dommett?'

'I thought you didn't know anything about him . . .'

'I don't. That was more than five years ago. He came to see me. I was living in Croydon at the time. Our eldest brother, Percy, had died and left a bit of money. There was only Harold and me left of us. He'd brought a paper for me to sign. We had a row then. I thought he was trying to do me out of part of my share. It didn't amount to much. It was chicken feed . . .'

The room was a shambles. There was an unmade bed in one corner, with the soiled bedclothes lying in a heap on

the floor and beside it a wash basin half-full of soapy water.
A few ramshackle chairs and a cheap table with the remnants of a meal scattered about it. There were a whisky
bottle and a dirty glass among the wreckage. Waddilove
half filled the glass and tossed it down.

'Well, why have you called on me? As I said, I know
nothing. All I can say is that if any money turns up, you
might let me know. I was his next-of-kin and he wasn't
married . . .'

'How do you know he wasn't married?'

Willy had a habit of inflating his cheeks and blowing
every now and then, and this, combined with his small red
nose, gave him the appearance of a circus clown.

'He wasn't the marrying sort . . .'

'He may have changed since last you saw him.'

'What did he die of?'

'Heart attack, I believe.'

'He must have left some money. I'll have to look into
that. Who's in charge of his affairs?'

'I've no idea. Mr. Dommett may have known, but as
he's dead – murdered – it's no use your going down to
Swinton, near where, by the way, I believe your brother was
buried.'

'So it's Dommett who's been murdered. Somebody
caught up with him at last, did they? I know the place. I
once went to see Harold down there. Family business. The
place was like a gaol. A wire fence all round it and a
savage dog prowling around. My brother had a real easy
job, sort of doing security work. Him and a little fellow
called Bugler were guards. Dommett seemed to have gone

off his head and was afraid of his own shadow, Harold said. I couldn't get any more than that out of him, but it seemed to me that somebody was out gunning for old Dommett. I wonder if Bugler knows who took charge of my brother's affairs. Do you have his address?'

'Bugler resigned his job just after your brother's death and left Dommett unprotected, if you like to describe it that way. The local police are investigating Dommett's death.'

Littlejohn wasn't going to give Willy Bugler's address. He had no wish to turn him loose on the surviving member of the Dommett trio.

'I'll have to go down to Swinton, won't I, if I want to look into Harold's affairs? The police there might be able to give me a tip about things. Are you from the local police?'

'No. I'm from Scotland Yard.'

'Was Dommett such a big shot that they've called Scotland Yard in about his murder?'

'No. I'm dealing with some inquiries at the London end of the case.'

'Where do I come in? I'd nothing to do with Dommett's murder. It's just wasting my time.'

'If you didn't know your brother was dead, this call, at least, has done some good. You might, as you say, come into some money now.'

'Yes; there's that about it, isn't there?'

'Where were you yesterday?'

Waddilove suddenly became aggressive.

'Look here, if you've called to mix me up in your

murder case you'd better think again. I was nowhere near the place. Swinton, wasn't it? I was nowhere near the place.'

' Where were you then?'

' Do I have to answer that?'

' Yes; here or at the police station.'

Littlejohn had had quite enough of the sordid squalor of the place. The window was closed and fastened and the air was foul, and, to make matters worse, Waddilove was drinking steadily from the bottle on the table.

' I think you'd better come with me to the station, Mr. Waddilove, before you're drunk. Leave the bottle alone until I've finished with you. Now, where were you all yesterday?'

The sharpness of Littlejohn's rebuke seemed to knock the stuffing out of Willy. He started to whine.

' I haven't refused to answer any of your questions, have I? You burst in on me and started to bully me, but I've been civil to you, haven't I? No need to run me in for that, have you? If you must know, I was here and about all yesterday. I'm a night watchman and I sleep most mornings. I was here in bed till noon. Then I had a meal and went out for some fresh air and a drink. I came back about four, packed my grub for the night, ate another meal, and then went on duty on my job at six. I was there all night till seven this morning . . .'

' That seems to cover it all, doesn't it, Mr. Waddilove? Have you anybody who can confirm it?'

Mr. Waddilove resented his veracity being questioned.

' Don't you believe me? Well, you can take it or leave it.

I don't care. You arrest me, if you like. You can't prove what I didn't do, can you?'

'Don't be silly, Mr. Waddilove. You arrived back from your job before eight, let us say, and you slept till noon. You must have handed over before you left. Who are your employers?'

'Steinthalls, the furriers, in Bond Street, but don't you go there inquiring about me. If the police turned up there asking questions I'd get the sack on the spot.'

'Did you see anybody here when you arrived back?'

'Yes. But I don't want to involve people living in this place. It'll get me a bad name.'

'Was it the lady in the room opposite?'

Willy hesitated.

'Yes. Cora's a well-brought-up lady and I won't have her mixed up with the police. It's not good enough.'

'How long were you together yesterday?'

'She gave me my breakfast when I got back here and she was around, here and in her own room, until I left shortly after four o'clock, and she'd packed my grub for the night.'

'You went out together for some fresh air and a drink, as you say? She was with you all the time?'

'Yes.'

'Very well. You say you don't want her mixed up with the police. We can settle this finally by your calling her in and asking her to confirm what you've told me.'

'She'll think I'm involved in this murder business and my name will be mud.'

'Call her in and see. Better still, we'll pay her a visit.'

Waddilove was about to protest, but Littlejohn took him

by the elbow, propelled him through his own doorway and across the landing. Then he gave Willy's arm a jerk and Willy, instead of knocking, gave a shout.

'Are you there, Cora? Can we come in?'

She had either got Willy well-trained or he was putting on his best behaviour to impress Littlejohn.

'Who's with you?'

'The police. They just want you to confirm . . .'

Presumably Waddilove was delaying matters to give Cora a chance of tidying up herself and the room, but she didn't seem to appreciate his tactics.

'Well what are you standing shouting there for? Come in the both of you.'

They entered, Willy pushing Littlejohn before him as though expecting an assault.

Cora was washed and neatly dressed, which made Willy look all the shabbier. The room, too, was plainly furnished but neat, with a bed in one corner all made and tidy. A table with a plastic cloth and a tea-set for two spread out on it. A geranium with a red flower on the window sill and a small table with a reading lamp and two armchairs in front of a gas fire.

The woman herself was buxom and of middle height. Dark, with jet-black hair and in her prime she must have been pretty. Now, she had a tired resigned look, as though she had given up battling with circumstances. What she saw in Willy was anybody's guess, but there is no accounting for taste. She had no eyes for Littlejohn, but a look, not of passion, but of motherly indignation for Willy, obviously her tallyman. She turned on him.

' Have you not washed and dressed yourself properly yet? And what are your braces doing hanging down? Pull them up and fasten them.'

She thought it was time she explained to Littlejohn and excused the pair of them.

' He works night, you know, and he's tired when he gets home. If I didn't look after him he'd go properly to seed. Before he met me he tried to commit suicide twice.'

Willy shrank under the scorn of his paramour until he looked like a large marionette manipulated from the ceiling by cords.

' I'm not feeling very well,' he said. ' The Inspector's brought me the news that my brother, Harold, is dead.'

' The police don't usually trouble themselves about births, marriages and deaths, unless a crime's been committed. Was your brother murdered, or something?'

' Not Harold. He died natural. It was his boss. He was murdered yesterday.'

' But you had nothing to do with that. You were here with me all day yesterday.'

Willy seemed quite surprised at this gratuitous confirmation of his alibi. He gave Littlejohn a look of triumph and straightened himself up and fastened his braces as if he'd received a tonic.

' By the way, what's happened to my brother's belongings? He must have had a lot of personal stuff at Dommett's place after all the time he'd been there.'

Willy said it truculently. His alibi had given him new confidence.

' I don't know. I agree there must have been quite an

accumulation of stuff at Swinton when he died. You'd better make some inquiries after Mr. Dommett's funeral. You know the address of his residence?'

' I've got it somewhere. As far as I can calculate, Harold died months ago. I wonder if Dommett collared all his stuff. It's scandalous that I haven't been informed before this.'

' That's your own fault. If you'd given your brother your present address it would probably have been found and you'd have been advised right away of his death.'

' Who's looking after Dommett's affairs now that he's dead?'

' He has a daughter living in Canada. She'll be informed and you'd better contact her when she comes over here.'

' You bet I will! What's her address?'

' I don't know. Now that I know where you are living I'll inform the local police and you'll be contacted in due course. Meanwhile keep away from Swinton. There's a murder investigation going on there and they'll have no time for you at present.'

' I don't care a damn. I've got my rights.'

' If you go there they'll send you packing. But please yourself. And now I must be going . . .'

Cora had been very quiet during the conversation and frowned as though she had something on her mind. She was standing in front of the gas fire which was set in the open fireplace. There was a small mantelpiece and fixed on the wall over it a large framed mirror, somewhat the worse for wear. Slipped under the edge of the frame were a number of postcards, presumably sent to Cora by friends on holidays at various resorts. Among them Littlejohn recognised one from Ilfracombe where he and his wife had briefly stayed during a recent tour of the west country. He strolled across and inspected it. Then he took it from the frame.

' Ilfracombe,' he said. ' We were there earlier this year. Very nice . . . Had you friends staying there?'

He glanced at the back of the card. It was addressed to Miss Cora Munroe, at the present address and bore a couple of lines in illiterate writing. *Arrived safe. No luck. Love. W.*

It was postmarked six months before and Littlejohn recollected that according to Bugler, Dommett had received a similar card from Ilfracombe.

Cora seemed quite pleased that Littlejohn had noticed the cards.

' Willy sent it. He'd been to Ilfracombe after a new job, but didn't get it . . .'

Through the mirror Littlejohn saw Willy make a quick impatient shake of his head to warn her to keep quiet.

' A day by the seaside. Did you like Scarborough as well as Ilfracombe, Mr. Waddilove?'

' I've never been to Scarborough . . .'

And he cast upon Cora another angry glare which she seemed puzzled to interpret.

' Have you forgotten, Willy? You went there, too, about a job.'

' You're mistaken. I never went about a job there.'

She flushed at the contradiction.

' You sent me a card from there. I've got it in the drawer.'

She made a move towards the cheap sideboard in the corner.

'The Inspector's wanting to get away. Leave it. It isn't worth arguing about...'

His anger gave him away.

'May I borrow this card, Miss Munroe?' said Littlejohn. 'I'd like to show it to my wife...'

It was a lame excuse, but he couldn't think of a better on the spur of the moment. Cora seemed a bit surprised, but agreed. Willy boiled over.

'Leave the damn thing where it was. You come here disturbing my sleep and asking silly questions and then you want to start disorganising the room. What good would a picture postcard do your wife, or you for that matter...'

Cora was flabbergasted.

'All this fuss about a postcard! It's mine and I can do as I want with it. And you did go to Scarborough...'

Willy was speechless with rage, but Littlejohn cut him short.

'Get properly dressed. I want you to come to Scotland Yard with me. We need your help with a murder case.'

'But I hadn't anything to do with Dommett's death. It's a scandal. Besides, I've got to get ready and go to work.'

'You're coming with me, so make yourself respectable. I'm not arresting you and I agree that you've probably nothing whatever to do with the crime. But you pretended you hadn't had contact with your brother for years and I don't believe you. Get moving, please.'

Cora looked bewildered.

'What is it all about? Surely the postcards...'

'Mr. Waddilove will tell you when he returns.'

'He'll soon be back?'

'Yes. We won't keep him long. We want to sort out some matters with him.'

'What about my job? I'll get the sack and you'll be responsible, Mister Inspector. I'll report you to your superiors for this.'

Willy kept reducing Littlejohn in rank, but Littlejohn let it pass. 'Miss Munroe will perhaps kindly telephone them. No need to mention the police. You can tell them he's unwell . . .'

'Again!' said Cora. 'Anyway, I'll do my best.'

It looked as though when Willy had drunk himself into an unfit condition to face his employers Cora had to make excuses for him!

Willy retired to the room across the landing and through the open doors punctuated his dressing with complaints and threats.

'I'll see my lawyer,' he said finally.

'You do that, Willy, and perhaps he'll be able to help you with your brother's estate as well.'

'Don't you call me Willy, either. Mister Waddilove to you.'

On the way out, after descending the seedy staircase, they met Mrs. Cuffright, who, thinking Willy was under arrest, denounced him from the steps with loud shouts and dramatic gestures.

'Don't come back,' she shouted and then, remembering that he hadn't paid the rent, she ran all the way upstairs to demand it from Cora.

6

Terror in the Night

P.C. BEESLEY, who arrived to relieve Plover at the manor, was a large, bluff, cheerful officer who prided himself on his common sense and physical strength, for he was one of the champion weight-lifters of the county. He was a sociable fellow and fond of talking and he was disturbed when he found that he was to keep his vigil alone.

The local force was short staffed and to add to the burdens of duty there had been a parliamentary by-election that day. The constituency was a scattered one, and there were five candidates. All day the squads of constables had kept order at the polling-stations and now, at nightfall, they became the guardians of the precious ballot boxes.

'I don't know why they pick on me for jobs like this,' Beesley told Plover. 'Why didn't they just lock the place up and be done with it? Nobody's going to run away with anything.'

'It's murder, though,' replied Plover. 'And there's a lot left undone. They'll have to go through the house for clues and fingerprints and as for the old ruin and the grounds . . . In my way of thinking, they'll never find out who did this. It might be gipsies, or a passing tramp, or an enemy of Dommetts. Like hunting for a needle in a haystack.'

'One thing's certain,' said Beesley. 'I'm not tramping about these grounds in the cold. I'm going to make myself comfortable in Dommett's house. The Super said it would be all right to do that. Have you got the key?'

Plover handed it over, but uttered a warning.

'It's said to be haunted, you know. This isn't the first murder that's took place here. One or two suicides as well. The last occupant of the old hall hung himself . .　　.'

'Oh, shut up! There's no such thing as haunting. It's in people's imagination. I'm going to make me a nice warm fire and take a little snooze when I feel like it. And they can haunt away to their heart's content. It won't bother me.'

'The only other person about is Grimes, the handyman. He's stone deaf and a bit potty. And he's got a savage wolfhound. So be careful.'

'You won't terrify me. Let's be getting across to the house. I'm due for relief at seven in the morning. The sergeant told me to tell you to report at the schoolroom at Little Grisby for the ballot boxes and then join the chaps who have to guard them all night at Midchester town hall.'

Plover could hardly contain himself.

'Why the hell do they need to have an election? They might as well make a present of the seat to the Tories. They always win.'

'Think of me, Sam, snug by the fire, while they're counting the votes . . .'

The pair of them set out for the house. They had to use their lamps as the whole place was lost in darkness.

' It makes my hair stand on end . . .'

' Don't be daft. I'll bet you ten bob it'll be as quiet as the grave all night long.'

P.C. Beesley did not know what was awaiting him.

Plover accompanied Beesley to the door of the house and then bade him goodnight and hurried away. The chill wind which frequently blew in the neighbourhood was rising and Beesley stood at the door awhile listening to its drumming along the ridge beyond the main road. Then he unlocked the door and switched on the light. The place was cold and silent except for the steady drip of a tap in the kitchen, the door of which stood open.

Beesley's hearty manner suddenly left him. He started to make a timid inspection of the place. He went to the kitchen door, switched on the light and looked round without moving, switched it off again and returned to the dining-room. He stood in the middle of the room turning his head from side to side and his eye falling on a well-kept welsh dresser, he crossed to it and began casually to open the drawers. He did it mechanically, taking no interest in the contents. Another door in one corner took his eye and he opened it. It led to the stairs and he shone his light up and down it, and then abandoned any idea of exploring in the dark. He took off his hat and coat and threw them on a chair and feeling the cold sought the means of keeping warm. There was plenty of wood and paper in the kitchen and he soon had a good fire roaring up the chimney of the dining-room. He opened his kit-bag and spread from it

large bags of sandwiches on the table. Finally, he produced
from his hold-all the delux vacuum flask his wife had given
him last Christmas, removed the cork and sniffed the
pleasant aroma of coffee with approval. At length he
began to eat his meal. It consisted of cold bacon and cheese,
but he, usually a hearty eater, took no interest in it. There
seemed to be an atmosphere of doom about the place which
sapped his energy and courage. Now and then, he stopped
his chewing and listened. He thought of Plover among his
votes and ballot boxes and wished he were there with him.

His meal finished, Beesley carefully wrapped up the
remnants and packed his bag again. The bracket clock on
the mantelpiece struck ten. Beesley wondered when his
seemingly endless vigil would end. There was an old copy of
The Times on the sideboard and he made up the fire and
settled in one of the easy chairs in front of it and began
to read half-heartedly. *Cypriot Acrobat Murders his
Partner. Churches to Help Third World* . . .

The clock was striking midnight when Beesley awoke.
His sleep had been so deep that it took him some time to
realise where he was and then he roused himself with a
start. He had to take a hold of himself for the mute oppres-
sive silence filled him with panic. He felt that the well-
lighted room was a sanctuary, whereas beyond the three
doors lay darkness and the terrors of the night. He realised
that it was part of his duty to patrol the place at least now
and then and he pulled himself together with a jerk and put
on his hat and coat. He was unarmed except for his trun-
cheon and he fingered it for comfort.

Beesley had drawn the curtains before eating his meal.

Now he pulled back those that covered the window overlooking the courtyard. He could see nothing at all beyond; the night seemed spread like another curtain on the other side of the glass. He went to the door, turned out the light and opened it. As his eyes got used to the dark he could make out the black silhouette of the great ruined house against the sky. The wind was still blowing on the ridge and the monotonous drumming persisted without disturbing the sheltered courtyard. He took his lamp and stepped out.

It took Beesley only a few moments to accustom himself to the darkness, but to him it seemed prolonged for hours. He felt an awful desire to shout as though gripped in a nightmare, and stifled it with an effort. He took a few steps across the yard, paved with hundreds of uniform-sized stones, over which he stumbled with groping feet, and then he lost sense of direction like someone adrift in a fog. Panic seized him so much that he forgot momentarily that he had a lamp in his hand. He switched it on.

Beesley revolved his lamp in a wide circle round the courtyard. It might have been originally constructed to defend the property and consisted of compact blocks of buildings on all four sides. Many of these were tumbling in disrepair. There was a great barn with its huge doors propped by large beams to keep them in place. Then a group of byres and the stables. Two sections of the latter had been converted into dwellings, one of which had been Dommett's house and the other, presumably empty, was awaiting an occupant. There was a gap between the barn and a large single-storeyed building. This had presumably been the main entrance of the compound, the massive door of which, at some time, had been torn from its hinges and was standing propped against the wall.

The constable made his way to the gateway feeling better for his preoccupation with his surroundings. He paused now and then to listen. Somewhere ahead of him an owl was hooting and a dog, far away, was barking. And in the background the gentle hum of the wind on the ridge. Beesley, a local countryman at heart, noted that the wind had changed direction from south to south-west, which meant rain.

He paused at the gateway and switched off his light. Outside the shelter of the compound the air around was cold and still. Beesley decided that he had patrolled far enough and thought again of the fire and the armchair in Dommett's house. He turned on his lamp again and lit up the ruined house and its barren trees from top to bottom. In his boyhood days he and the gang of village lads of which he was a member had often cycled there and fought battles and played violent games among the forsaken rooms and passages. To Beesley, the place had decayed so rapidly, that he hardly recognised it. Years ago the windows had been without glass, but now the very stone frames had been smashed and their remnants hung round the frontage like rotten teeth in a wide gaping mouth.

Beesley remembered Miss Mowll, the last of her family, living in the remaining two habitable rooms of the manor house, an old woman clad in voluminous black, who used to appear and chase him and his comrades about the ruins, brandishing an ebony walking-stick. She had lived there in the company of Blaster, once a young handsome footman at the hall and finally, with the fall of the family, the sacristan and gravedigger of the church which was then in active use. It was said they had been lovers, but before they could marry it was disclosed that Matthew Blaster was the illegitimate son of Miss Mowll's father, which appalling revelation had driven the pair of them out of their wits. After her father's suicide she and Blaster had lived together among the ruins of the old home until Blaster died and now his grave in the forlorn burial place of the church was the only place kept tidy and covered in flowers all the year round, the handiwork of Grimes.

As Beesley turned to leave the ruins behind him, he grew alert again, stiffened and listened. The hair rose on the back of his neck and then he realised that this was no ghostly noise. Someone was digging in the garden at the side of the house, a few acres of ground formerly used for raising vegetables and flowers. In its better days it had been protected by thick box hedges and hazel trees, but now they had degenerated into an almost impassable barrier and the beds were smothered in grass and weeds.

Beesley tiptoed silently across the cobbled yard in the direction of the sound and at length made out a light shining dimly through the bushes. It came from a storm lantern standing on the ground which dimly illuminated a kneeling figure busily exploring a hole he had dug in the soil. As Beesley watched, the man found what he had been seeking and drew it from the earth. It was an object wrapped up in cloth which the intruder eagerly removed. Beesley strained his eyes to identify it and finally succeeded. It was a double-barrelled shot-gun.

The constable was in a dilemma. He did not know whether or not the weapon was loaded and what were his chances of reaching the man before he had time to use it. On the other hand, the stranger was unaware of his presence there and that might give Beesley the necessary advantage. He decided to attack.

The man was by now on his feet examining his find with apparent admiration. He turned it over several times and then broke the breach and squinted down the barrels at the lamplight. Then Beesley could hear the snap-snap of the firing pin as he tried the trigger. The constable sighed with relief. At least the gun was not loaded. The man was like a child with a new toy. He closed the breach with a flourish raised the gun to his shoulder, tested the balance, tossed it from hand to hand and then placed it carefully on the ground and started to fill in the hole.

Beesley, who had meanwhile been cautiously forcing his way through the bramble thicket had reached the open on the other side. He decided it was now time to make his move. He laid his lamp on the ground, gathered his strength, and launched himself in a low tackle and before he realised what was happening took the visitor above the knees. The pair of them crashed to the ground. Overhead the rooks, alarmed by the noise, flapped their wings in the tops of the elm trees.

The policeman was athletic and in good form, but found at once that he had taken on as much, if not more, than he could handle. His adversary made a quick recovery and soon they were locked together in a grim battle. In the scuffle the lamp was overturned and extinguished.

Beesley was a champion wrestler and weight-lifter in the locality but here he found a technique quite foreign to his own. The stranger performed like a great bear, hugging Beesley to his flabby body with his powerful arms. The policeman, winded by the unexpected onset, found his chest constricted like a pair of closed bellows and his eyes protruded from his head in the mighty effort he was making to release himself. Fear seized him lest he should be unable to break the lock in which he was held. His opponent groaned and snorted from his efforts; Beesley had no breath left with which to make any noise at all.

Then, as though the stranger suddenly grew afraid, he relaxed his hold. All the strength seemed to ebb from him and he sagged to the ground and lay there like a defeated animal awaiting the end. Neither of them spoke at first; they were too busy recovering their breath. The intruder remained on the ground just as he had fallen there. Beesley relieved at the change of events, assisted him to his feet.

' What the hell do you think you're doing?' he said.

It was a stupid question in the circumstances, but Beesley felt he must say something if only to hear the man speak. Instead, there was no answer.

' I'm deaf,' said the man.

It only needed that to complete the nightmare. In the pitch darkness, after a deathly scuffle, and now no means of communication! And then to add to it all, someone was floundering among the neglected bushes and brandishing a lighted torch in the direction of where Beesley and his captive were standing like two statues.

' Is there anybody there?'

Beesley almost wept with relief. It was P.C. Plover.

'Is that you, Fred?' he shouted.

Plover's torch shone across the forsaken garden, lighting up the shabby statue of a nymph without head and one arm, and a broken sundial. Finally, the beam picked out Beesley and his prisoner, standing side by side expectantly, and revealed the latter's identity. It was Grimes, the gardener, whose face wore a vacant expression as though he had not yet recovered from his nocturnal adventure and he still wondered what it was all about.

'What have you two been up to?'

Plover seemed as bewildered as Grimes.

'It's a good job you've turned up, Fred. I found this fellow digging up a gun which I guess he'd hidden. I'll bet it belonged to Dommett. He always carried a gun and it was missing when his body was found.'

'His name's Grimes. He's stone deaf and a bit woolly in his wits ...'

'I know him now that you've lit him up, Fred,' said Beesley. 'I surprised him here when I did my rounds. He fought like a tiger. He's as strong as an ox ...'

Not to be outdone by Beesley's mixed metaphors, Plover continued to discuss Grimes's reputation.

'It's said locally that Grimes is the illegitimate son of the last of the Mowll family who were once lords of the manor here. You remember Miss Mowll, don't you? There's a sort of legend about her. She had a love affair with a footman or a gamekeeper or something ...'

Then they remembered Grimes patiently waiting in his silent world for something to happen.

'What are we going to do about him? He seems mild enough now.'

'You should have seen him just before you arrived. Went absolutely berserk. I must admit I surprised him, and I'll bet he was as scared as I was.'

'I was passing the gate and thought I'd call to see how you were getting along. Colonel Foster-Revington won the seat in the election by 15 votes. There were two recounts, otherwise I wouldn't have been up at this unearthly hour.'

'What time is it?'

'Two o'clock.'

Beesley picked up the gun gingerly.

'Better handle this carefully, just in case there are prints on it. I wonder if Dommett was killed by a blow from this gun. We didn't find any weapons, you know.'

Beesley held the weapon under Plover's lamp and read the name of a famous gunsmith on the barrels. He whistled.

'This isn't the sort of gun a fellow like Grimes would own. It must have belonged to Dommett. I wonder how much Grimes knows about the murder. He might have got in an argument with Dommett and gone berserk like he did with me. Let's go back to the house and we'll decide what to do then. In any case, we'd better ring headquarters and get Superintendent Winstanley out here.'

Grimes was quite docile now and shambled along between the two constables and entered the house with them as though he had business there and wished to get it over. They tried to hold a conversation with him, but even loud shouts made no impression on him. Now and then he nodded and smiled in what appeared to be a gesture of his goodwill. He was not even alarmed about his predicament and seemed to have forgotten all about the gun. Finally, he spoke. It took the two officers by surprise; as if a dog had suddenly started to articulate.

' Can I sit down? Can I have a smoke?'

Beesley who seemed eager to appease Grimes, hastily offered him a cigarette. Grimes smiled and shook his head.

' Pipe,' he said and took a battered object from his pocket, inspected the dottle, and lit it and puffed out noisesome smoke with great relish.

Beesley felt well satisfied with Grimes's behaviour. He had anticipated a further eruption and perhaps another fight and then he and Plover having to tie up Grimes pending the arrival of a vehicle to take him to gaol. As it was, Grimes seemed settled for the rest of the night.

' Do you think I ought to let the Super. know now?' Beesley said to Plover.

' Yes. Right away.'

' It'll mean getting him up out of bed . . .'

' So what? This is important. It might turn out that Grimes killed Mr. Dommett, although, somehow, I don't think he did. But if he did do it, we'd get in a hell of a row if we sat it out till somebody turned up in the morning . . .'

Beesley seemed impressed by his colleague's rambling argument and made for the telephone. He stood in front of the instrument for some time putting his thoughts in order and mentally rehearsing what he would say. Then he dialled headquarters and told his tale. He recited it as though he were facing the magistrate with Grimes in the dock. Sometimes he waxed eloquent, especially about the fight in the dark and the discovery of the gun. He finally exaggerated a bit, ending by saying that he and P.C. Plover had detained Grimes and were now awaiting further orders.

The night sergeant, who had been dozing, received the news without enthusiasm.

'You haven't charged Grimes, have you?'

'No.'

'You'd better not. He's deaf as a board and will need careful handling. I'll report right away to the Chief. He's sure to be coming over there right away, although he won't be pleased about being roused from his bed. He was here till half-past two attending to the election . . . Don't do anything till he arrives . . .'

'What's all that about?' asked Plover, who had been listening to the rigmarole.

'It's only Sergeant Puddiphat trying to teach us our business. Johnny Know-all wants to know if we've charged Grimes. As if we would! He must be drunk. He's informing the Super at once. So I expect Winstanley will be here in about half-an-hour. While we're waiting for him what about trying to communicate with Grimes? I wonder if he can read.'

Beesley crossed to the dresser and opened the drawers one after another until he found a writing-pad and a ball-point pen. Then he tackled Grimes.

'Can you read?' he shouted at the top of his voice. Grimes, as usual pointed to one ear.

'I'm deaf. I can't hear you.'

Beesley scribbled his question on the pad and thrust it under Grimes's nose.

Grimes was either a poor reader or else was being awkward. He said nothing but pondered the writing with his mouth open.

'I can't read this.'

So Beesley carefully printed the question and tried again. Grimes seemed delighted with the result and replied at once.

'Yes. I went to school.'

Then followed an inquisition, Beesley laboriously printing his questions and Grimes enthusiastically shouting back his answers. Now and then P.C. Plover added a comment to show he was interested.

'Tell him he's no need to shout the house down . . .'

'Better not. If we start messing him about, he'll probably dry-up altogether.'

Beesley continued. 'You know, don't you, that you could go to prison for attacking a policeman?'

'I didn't attack you. You started it.'

One up for Grimes! P.C. Plover chuckled.

Beesley thought he'd better abandon that part of the inquiry.

'Where did you get the gun?'

'Mr. Dommett gave it to me.'

'That's not true. He'd never give away a gun like that. It's worth hundreds of pounds.'

' I don't know anything about that. He gave it me.'

' You found it in the spinney, didn't you? So you took it and hid it.'

' When I heard the boss was dead I knew they'd take his gun away from me, so I hid it.'

' Did you see Mr. Dommett lying dead by the side of his gun when you found it?'

' No. I didn't. He gave it to me before then.'

' Don't tell me any more lies, Grimes. The truth will come out and then it will be worse for you.'

Grimes dried up and retired into his silent world again. Beesley realised that all this would have to be gone through again, officially, so abandoned the matter of the gun. It was a long-drawn-out inquiry and meanwhile Plover had been pottering about, re-lighting the fire and making tea. He handed out two cups for Beesley and Grimes. It was a gesture like pouring oil on troubled waters and the dialogue was resumed.

' Where were you yesterday morning?'

' At Barsby.'

' What were you doing there?'

' Putting up stalls and tents for the fair.'

' What time did you go there?'

' After breakfast.'

' Did you see Mr. Dommett before you left?'

' No. There was nobody about. I asked Mr. Dommett the day before if I could be away for the day of the fair. He said no. With Mrs. Batt off shopping, Waddilove dead, and Bugler given in his notice and left, that would leave the boss alone if I was away. He didn't like being alone . . .'

' But you went to the fair all the same?'

' Yes. I'd promised the reverend Beecham I'd be at the fair and do the jobs as asked. So I went. Had to walk it. There being nobody there to drive the car. I never saw Mr. Dommett alive again.'

' What time did you reach Barsby?'

' Nine o'clock.'

' How did you know the time?'

' I looked at my watch . . .'

He produced an old-fashioned silver watch like a turnip from his fob-pocket and proudly showed it to Beesley.

' . . . I work by the hour for my pay.'

' How long were you there?'

' They gave me my dinner; 'am sandwiches, buns and tea. I finished in time for the start of the fair. Half-past two. A shillin' an hour. Five-and-a-half hours, less a half for dinner, five shillin's.'

' Who found you the job?'

' Mr. Beecham, the vicar. I always do it. Done it for 20 years. I'm the best tent and stall putter-up in the district. I'm handy with heavy things, you see.'

Beesley, from experience, did not challenge Grimes's feats of strength.

P.C. Plover growled to himself.

' I'd been thinking Grimes might have killed Dommett to get his gun, or perhaps for some personal reason or quarrel and that we'd got the case sewed-up. But if the Rev. Beecham confirms what Grimes has told us, he'll have a cast-iron alibi. He was at Barsby all the time Dommett was getting himself murdered.'

Beesley had laboriously written down the questions and answers and thought he had enough information for a preliminary inquiry. He put his papers in order ready for the Chief when he arrived.

' We'd better have your name and address, Grimes.'

' Jason Grimes, Manor Cottage, Swinton Lazars.'

' Jason . . . that's an unusual name.'

Grimes pulled himself up proudly and began to intone his credentials.

' Everything's unusual about me. I never had a proper name. I was found as a baby on the church doorstep here. Nobody knew who my parents were and never found out. The Reverend Jason Luck, the vicar at the time, gave me his name when he christened me. Where he got Grimes from I never knew. Miss Mowll, then lady of the manor, paid for my keep till I could earn my own living and I was brought up by Will Bull, the blacksmith, and his wife. I lost my hearing when I got the measles . . .'

The arrival of Winstanley cut short the rest of the story of Grimes's life.

7

Fear Round About

WILLY WADDILOVE seemed to have given up the struggle and hardly spoke a word on the way to Scotland Yard. Littlejohn did not encourage him to talk. He preferred, now that Willy had obviously been lying, to interrogate him on his own ground.

Now and then Willy gave him a sulky look and, as they neared The Yard, he suddenly grew alive again.

'What's this all about?' he said aggressively, as though awakening to the idea that he might be in danger of getting mixed up in a murder case.

'We'd better wait until we get indoors. You can gather your thoughts better there.'

Willy didn't see the point.

'I've no thoughts to gather together on this murder business. Are you arresting me?'

'No. You're just going to assist us with our inquiries.'

'I never even saw Dommett, let alone murder him. As for what you say about assisting the police, from what I see in the newspapers, you usually land in the dock. I want a lawyer . . .'

'No need for that. It would be useless expense.'

The car drew up and Littlejohn shepherded Willy to his

room. Soon they were sitting face to face with cups of tea in front of them.

'What's this for?' asked Willy ungraciously. 'I don't like tea, in any case.'

'Sorry. There's nothing else. You can't expect champagne cocktails to celebrate your visit, can you?'

'You've brought me a long way for nothing and at the same time made me risk losing my job for absence. I don't know a thing about Dommett or how he and my brother got along. Besides, Harold died weeks before Dommett did. I don't see how Harold's connected with the murder either.'

'I've brought you here because you didn't tell me the truth when we were at your place.'

Willy was about to protest, but Littlejohn cut him short.

'It's useless your saying you didn't try to deceive me into believing that you and your brother were like two strangers. I'll bet you were as thick as thieves. You met now and then, if not frequently. You even went to the extent of posting cards for him to Dommett from seaside places you visited. The cards were anonymous and abusive. Why did you send them?'

'I don't know what you're talking about. Why should I send cards to Dommett? You must be joking.'

'Don't let's beat about the bush any further. You know I have in my pocket a card you sent to Miss Munroe from Ilfracombe. You posted a similar one to Dommett and another from Scarborough in the same abusive terms. We know you sent both cards. Why?'

Willy licked his dry lips. He was feeling the need of a drink.

'It was a joke.'

'A poor sort of a joke, wasn't it? To call a man a bastard and to hint that you were on his trail to do him harm.'

Willy suddenly grew serious and assumed an earnest look.

'I do assure you, Inspector . . .'

'For the record, Willy, I'm Chief Superintendent . . .'

'Blimey! Harold must have been in something serious to be mixed up with Scotland Yard top brass. But I do assure you, sir, there was no 'int of doing Dommett harm. Harold and me did make contact now and then and on those two occasions I happened to mention where I was going. He suggested I wrote and posted cards to Dommett for a joke. Just a joke . . .'

'Don't keep talking about jokes. It was damned serious and you know it. What was your brother up to?'

'I don't know. I swear it.'

'Was it some sort of blackmail?'

Willy looked hurt.

'I'm surprised at you suggesting such a thing. Why should we do that?'

'You tell me. You can also tell me exactly what occurred between you and your brother when this postcard affair started. Take your time, but remember that you're obstructing the police and that's an offence.'

'I've got to get back to my work . . .'

Willy was beginning to perspire freely and ran his finger between his throat and his soiled collar to ease the tension.

'If you're so eager to get back on the job, you'd better tell me everything and then you can go.'

'There's nothing in it. Harold called at my place one day when he was in London . . .'

'I thought you'd more or less lost touch with one another.'

'That was true. We had. I'd written to him, however. I was out of a job and needed a loan to repay a debt. He called and helped me out.'

'Why didn't you tell me that at first? Can you wonder that I can't trust you to help us?'

Willy beat on the desk with both fists.

'Will you stop needling me? I'm telling you the truth now. He called, and in the course of conversation I happened to mention I was going to Scarborough next day about a job in an hotel. It was then he suggested the joke about the postcards. He told me what to put on it. After that he called again to get the money he'd lent me and I couldn't find it but told him I was in for a job in Ilfracombe. He asked me to send another card the same as before . . .'

'Why was he doing this?'

'I told you, it was a joke.'

'Are you sure you haven't any more information about your brother that you think I ought to know?'

'Why should I keep it back? Harold was never a confiding sort. He lived a life of his own and kept his business to himself.'

'Did you repay the money he lent you?'

'No. I never had any luck with money. But I guess it

doesn't matter now. Unless Harold has made a will leaving his money to some woman or other, it'll come to me now, won't it?'

'I can't help you there. You'd better make inquiries yourself.'

'Where?'

'Perhaps he had a lawyer. If not, I guess the public trustee will be handling it. Your own lawyer could see to it, if you have one.'

'What would I be doing having a lawyer? However, I know a chap who's as good as any lawyer. I'll see him about it.'

Willy rose to his feet and stretched himself. He seemed more cheerful perhaps at the thought of the fortune to come.

'Can I go now?'

'Yes.'

'Don't you send people like me, who call to help the police, back home in an official car?'

Willy tried to appear nonchalant by taking a drink of the cold tea in his cup and then lighting a cigarette.

'I'm sorry, we're economising, Willy.'

'All right, then. I don't bear you any ill-will. If I come into a fortune from Harold I'll stand you a drink.'

And with that he departed in high spirits. Littlejohn was sure Willy was relieved at not being pressed for further information which he felt he was able to give.

Littlejohn rang Winstanley and arranged to meet him at Swinton Lazars next morning.

'Mrs. Batt is coming to the house for the rest of her

belongings tomorrow,' Winstanley told him. 'I think we'd better pump her for some more information . . .'

* * *

At eight o'clock the following morning Littlejohn set out on his journey. It was warm and sunny but as he ascended from the main highway through the network of minor roads the temperature gradually fell and when he reached Cold Barsby he found the village living up to its reputation. On the outskirts of the place he came upon the vicar striding out, in spite of his age and corpulence, on his parochial visits.

'Good morning, sir,' said Littlejohn. 'Can I give you a lift?'

Mr. Beecham stopped and peered blankly through his spectacles. His mind had been fixed on his many children and he was wondering whether they were a blessing or a chastisement. Two of them had just started with whooping-cough and had kept him awake all night. The scourge would probably run through the other three of them and build up a small orchestra of whoopers and coughers. Added to that misfortune, another of his brood had developed a mania for striking matches and had already started a number of small fires in the vicarage.

'I seem to know you . . .'

Mr. Beecham raised his hand.

'Don't tell me,' he said. 'My memory for names is failing and I must not encourage it . . . Littlejohn! That's it!'

And he wrung Littlejohn's hand warmly as though the Chief Superintendent had done him a great favour. Then he climbed nimbly into the car.

'Very good of you to offer me a lift. I've a call to make in Ashby Newbold and would welcome a ride there.'

The good man must have imagined Littlejohn was plying for hire, for Littlejohn was sure he'd passed through the village about three miles back. He did not argue, however, but turned the car and they started off again.

Although the vicar's mind was defective in the matter of names it was otherwise quite bright and almost at once he began to talk of the local murder.

'You are, I suppose, Chief Superintendent, here about the awful crime committed at Swinton Lazars. I hear you were the first to find the dead body. Poor Mr. Dommett. The whole matter is copiously dealt with in the morning papers. The locality is filled with reporters and I hear that a team of television men is at Swinton gathering information and pictures for the evening broadcast. It gives the whole locality an evil reputation. Several reporters called on me this morning, but I was able to send them off without an interview. My children have the whooping cough and when I told the gentlemen of the press they seemed to lose their enthusiasm and went hurriedly away.'

'Would you have been able to give them any useful information otherwise, sir?'

They had already reached the outskirts of Ashby Newbold and the vicar consulted his watch.

'Thanks to your kindly giving me a lift, Chief Superintendent, I have half-an-hour to spare. If you will stop the car I will be able to tell you what I know. I might help you in your inquiries.'

To avoid blocking the narrow road entirely Littlejohn drew up in a gateway. Mr. Beecham removed the black woollen gloves he was wearing and rubbed his hands together to restore circulation.

'I have been uneasy in my mind for a long time about Mr. Dommett and his affairs. It was a kind of premonition. I think I told you before that he dismissed me rudely when I called on him at the manor. I have had little to do with him since. He did, however, ring me on the telephone some time ago. Did you know he had two men, whom for lack of a better word I will call manservants? They were more like bodyguards and he was never seen about the locality without them. True, one of them was his chauffeur and drove him about in an old car and the other sat by his side like a footman. But one had a feeling that they were like those shadowy grim men who accompany foreign potentates on diplomatic visits and see that nobody shoots them. But I am doing all the talking, Mr. Littlejohn. Do you wish to ask me any questions?'

Mr. Beecham lapsed into contemplation and muttered to himself.

'Vessel of wrath? Devil's disciple . . .?'

'I beg your pardon . . .'

'Please forgive me. I was seeking a word which would describe Mr. Dommett. There is an expression, but it has slipped my memory. Pray go on. I will not interrupt again.'

'You were saying, sir, that Mr. Dommett spoke to you over the phone recently.'

'Ah yes. The large man was the chauffeur and the small round one was the footman. When Dommett rang me up, the large one had died and Dommett wanted permission to have him buried in the churchyard at Swinton Lazars. I informed him that we had long since ceased to inter the dead in the graveyard there but that, subject to the usual formalities, the graveyard at Cold Barsby was available. He seemed irritated and inclined to argue but I remained firm and he finally agreed. So we buried Mr. Waddington . . .'

'Waddilove . . .'

'Eh? Yes. We buried him at Cold Barsby. It was a strange funeral. Mr. Meals, our village undertaker, took charge. Mr. Dommett objected to that, at first. He seemed to think Mr. Waddington could just be packed in a box and buried without more ado, like a dead cat or a dog. I rebuked him. He did not attend the funeral. He doesn't believe in God and raised objections to Christian burial. I quickly told him we were concerned not with Dommett's immortal soul but that of Mr. Waddington and I insisted on the usual rites. I wonder now how Mr. Sebastian Dommett is faring, so violently called to the judgement seat. Eventually, the funeral took place at Cold Barsby, with Mr. Meals, myself and the little round man, Mr. Trumpeter . . .'

'Mr. Bugler . . .'

'I knew it was a brass musical instrument . . . Yes, Bugler is right. He attended.'

'Did you have much conversation with him?'

'Not really. He seemed too upset for sociability. He even wept. He must have been very fond of Mr. Waddington . . .'

'Did you see the death certificate?'

'Yes. Mr. Meals showed it to me. Death due to coronary occlusion. Mr. Bugler said Mr. Waddington had suffered previous attacks and that his death was not unexpected. The doctor said the same and there was no reason for an inquest.'

'Who signed the death certificate?'

'Dr. Calderwood, of Ashby Newbold. His surgery is just along the main street there. You'll probably find him in if you wish to see him.'

Mr. Beecham took out his watch and looked at it as though he couldn't believe his eyes.

'Is there anything else, Mr. Littlejohn. I must be off to my meeting in five minutes. It is a diocesan affair and the Venerable Archdeacon is to address us on the Church and the Common Market. I must not be late.'

Littlejohn felt that, given time, Mr. Beecham might give him more help, but to hurry him might add to the confusion.

'I'll run you down to your meeting-place.'

'The village hall, right opposite Dr. Calderwood's. It is very good of you. Had things been normal I'd have asked you to tea at the vicarage, but the prevailing epidemic of whooping-cough makes such gatherings impossible at the moment. By the way, do you know a good remedy for whooping-cough, Chief Superintendent? Dr. Calderwood's medicine doesn't seem to make the slightest impression . . .'

Littlejohn remembered how, in the past, one of his wife's daily helps had, after three weeks' whooping by her three children, been saved from madness by a neighbour's recommendation.

'Get some mouse-ear . . . it's a herb . . . from a herbalist and try it out as he recommends . . .'

Mr Beecham looked a bit dubious.

'Mouse-ear? One can try anything and I must confess my poor wife and I are in extremis . . .'

He took it down on an old envelope from his pocket.

'Pray don't mention this to Dr. Calderwood if you are calling on him. He gets very annoyed at what he calls old women's remedies. I must leave you now, Mr. Littlejohn. If I can be of further help, telephone me. If the mouse-ear is effective we may yet have our little tea at the vicarage. By the way, did I tell you I think Mr. Dommett was afraid of something? Terribly afraid. I have remembered the expression I was seeking to describe Mr. Dommett. It comes from the Book of Jeremiah . . .'

Mr. Beecham gathered himself together to pronounce the oracle.

'The Lord hath not called thy name Pashur but Magor-Missabib: Fear Round About,' he intoned. And with that he rushed across the road to embrace the Venerable Archdeacon who was making signals of goodwill in his direction.

Littlejohn turned the car and hurried away to meet Winstanley at the manor house, as arranged. Mrs. Batt, who was due to arrive to collect her belongings, had not yet arrived. Winstanley had much to report that did not contribute much to the case.

'There was a by-election here yesterday and left us short of staff. However, we had a squad of men out on the murder case inquiring about strangers in the locality. They drew a complete blank. The fair at Cold Barsby kept a lot of the locals busy and became the alibi of most of the parish inhabitants. So far, no strangers are reported and the one family of gipsies camped hereabouts on the old Gartree Road gave a good account of themselves. They were all women and children; the two men of the party, who are usually well-behaved, got drunk a couple of nights ago, stole some chickens and were in prison in Midchester while Dommett was being murdered.'

He went on to tell Littlejohn about Beesley's adventures with Grimes the night before and the recovery of Dommett's gun.

' I might have suspected Grimes, but he's got a cast-iron alibi for the time of the crime. He's changed his story about the gun several times. First he said that Dommett gave it to him; which is ridiculous. It's a top-ranking weapon worth, at a guess, £500. Dommet would never have given it away.'

' And the alibi . . .?'

' Beesley, after trying without success to get a proper tale out of Grimes by shouting, hit upon the idea of communicating in writing and it came off. Grimes was at Cold Barsby from early morning until after lunchtime helping to set up the stalls for the fair and the vicar, Mr. Beecham, confirms that. When he returned home Grimes must have come upon the dead body of Dommett with the gun lying beside it and taken and buried the gun. He's not very bright and would never have thought he might be found out. He'd apparently wiped and cleaned it before hiding it and made a thorough job of it. Superficially, it bears only

Grimes's prints, but we've sent it to the path. lab. for examination. They may find something that we've missed.'

'Did you get anything else out of him about the life they led at the manor and Dommett's share of it?'

'Not a thing about it. He's not actually mad; just stupid and slow. He was a foundling, said to be the son, on the wrong side of the blanket, of one of the Mowll family who were once lords of the manor here. Mrs. Dommett was a distant cousin, the last of the line. That's how they got this place. The only friend Grimes seems to have is a large Alsatian dog, which since it attacked one of our men searching the spinney for clues, has been shut in at Grimes's cottage. It seems to have been one of the squad of Dommett's bodyguards when he was alive.'

Littlejohn reported the results of his visits to Bugler and Willy Waddilove. The abusive postcards puzzled them both.

'I think I'd better make another call on Bugler and see if he knows about those cards. I don't trust him. He's too evasive and slippery. He has an alibi of sorts. His sister, with whom he lives, will confirm that he was at home in Wimbledon at the time of the crime. Whether she's dependable or not I don't know, but I'm sure she will support Bugler in anything he says.'

'We went through the contents of Dommett's desk. I thought we might have got a lead there one way or another. But Dommett didn't seem to be one for collecting papers. There was nothing much there, except routine bills and details and plans of repairs and improvements he had in mind for the manor property. There's a safe, too. The key was on Dommett's key-ring. The safe was one of the type you could almost get in with a tin-opener. There was just over £100 in cash there, some account books and bank statements and a copy of Dommett's will. He left all he had to Mrs. Batt.'

' Nothing to his daughter?'

' Not a cent. He's cut her off properly.'

' What was the date of the will?'

' Last week. It seems to me that after the domestic upheaval of Bugler and Waddilove leaving his employ he made a new will. Being a lawyer, he'd apparently drawn it up himself and had it witnessed at the bank and he made the bank his trustee.'

' Where did he bank?'

' Garfitt's Bank at Ashby Newbold.'

' Have you spoken to the manager there?'

' Only to inform him formally of the death. I told him we'd be calling to see him in a day or two.'

' Would you like me to do it?'

' I was hoping you would, Tom. I'm pulled out of the place at present.'

' All right. I'll go after lunch after we've had another talk with Mrs. Batt. When do you expect her?'

' Her brother-in-law has a car and she's arranged for him to bring her over from Burton Masterton before lunch. Knowing that car, I suggested we might send a police car to pick her up, but she didn't like the idea at all. She said people would think we'd arrested her. We've had her brother-in-law in court three times for driving a defective vehicle and I guess this is a gesture of defiance on his part.

However, if the car doesn't disintegrate altogether I suppose we'll see them before nightfall . . .'

But his moment of triumph was on the way for Herbert Tidy, Mrs. Batt's brother-in-law. Hardly had Winstanley finished running down him and his vehicle than he arrived with his wife, her sister, a large shaggy dog and a cat asleep in a cat-basket all in a new red racing car from which he coaxed as much noise as possible to attract the attention of the police. He had not even time to greet them.

'What do you think of the new car, eh? Won it in a competition on the telly.'

8

The Opinions of Mrs. Lucy Batt

THE ARRIVAL of Herbert Tidy and his retinue was an embarrassment. The proprietor of a grocer's shop in Burton Masterton, he had recently suffered the appearance in the town of a large competing supermarket and calculated that before long he would be bankrupt. In the resulting depressed condition, the idea of taking flight with a girl in the church choir he greatly admired, or even of committing suicide, had crossed his mind. Then his wife had bullied him into a television *Brain of the Midlands* contest. Herbert was eminently suited for such an ordeal. For years he had made up his declining grocery profits by entering competitions in newspapers, magazines, or sponsored by the purveyors of various goods he sold in his shop. Thus he had accumulated a fund of strange information which served him well as he ploughed his way to fame and fortune.

Now, the proud winner of a splendid new car and £300 in cash, he was sure his luck had changed and his spirits and his opinions of himself had risen considerably.

'I'll run you over to Swinton in the car,' he told Mrs. Batt. 'With me to advise you, you won't need a lawyer.

I've had experience of the police and I'll see that they don't try any tricks on you.'

He arrived at the manor house, which he had never visited before, full of his own importance until he saw the battered premises, when his spirits fell.

'Why! The whole place is in ruins. If as you said, Lucy, he's probably included you in his will, you're inheriting not a fortune but a liability. We've got to be careful. I'm surprised you stayed on here. You must have been out of your mind . . .'

'And the only woman about the place with four men,' said her sister, not to be outdone by the Brain.

Herbert was a small man with a large bald head and protruding eyes and normally had the unctuous manners of a small shopman ingratiating his best customers. Now his unction vanished and he grew aggressive.

'Let me do the talking,' he told the women. 'We're standing no nonsense.'

Right away he singled out Winstanley and told him why he was there.

'I represent my sister-in-law, a widow, and I'm here to advise her. She knows nothing whatever about the crime, being absent about her business when it occurred. She's here to help the police, not to get herself involved or accused.'

Winstanley cleared the decks right away.

'Of course, sir, we appreciate your help, but there is no point in a third party intervening at present. We simply wish to ask Mrs. Batt a few questions about the life they led here before the murder. Your presence will not be required at the interview. It would only complicate matters. Might I suggest that you, Mr. . . . Mr. . . .'

'The name's Tidy . . .'

'Oh, you're the man who won the *Brain of the Midlands* competition . . . Congratulations. May I suggest, Mr. Tidy, that you show your wife round the estate until we've finished our business.'

'I h'object!' said Mr. Tidy with emphasis.

'I'm sorry, sir, but if you don't do as we wish we'll have to adjourn to the police station in Midchester, which would be very awkward, wouldn't it?'

He gave Mr. Tidy a suave smile and Mr. Tidy had nothing to say. He had been in the police station several times and had no wish to visit it again, even in his elegant new car.

'All right. You hold all the tricks. My wife and me will go for a run in the car. But under protest. Make a note of that. Under protest.'

He then explained the situation to Mrs. Batt, warned her to be careful what she said and looked at his new watch, purchased to celebrate his winnings.

'It is now 11.45. I will return in one hour to pick up Mrs. Batt and take her to lunch and will expect her to be ready.'

His wife, a very large woman who had remained vigilantly in the front seat of the car with the cat clinging precariously to her enormous frontage, felt herself called upon to endorse her husband's decision.

'Quarter to one, Lucy. Remember that. And don't let the police take advantage of you.'

Whereat, the cat, awakened by the shouting, leapt from the car, flattened its ears, and fled into the spinney.

'Now look what you've done,' said Mrs. Tidy to Winstanley and she panted off in search of the truant, calling her husband and the dog to follow her in the hunt, which lasted until well after the interview with Mrs. Batt had terminated.

Mrs. Batt, disgusted at the commotion, remained unperturbed and made her way to her old living quarters without a look behind. Instead of the natty new car, Herbert Tidy had been offered a colour television, an automatic washer and a refrigerator and Mrs. Batt was strongly of the opinion that he ought to have chosen the three domestic appliances. 'He ought to have considered his wife and family,' she told Littlejohn in a burst of confidence. 'I told him so. Since when he hasn't spoken a civil word to me.'

Winstanley was anxious to interview Mrs. Batt before the Tidys returned from hunting the cat. The dog, which seemed to have taken possession of the car, remained asleep in it yapping with pleasure at his dreams. Mrs. Batt insisted on making cups of tea before being interrogated and after that was only with difficulty persuaded to talk before departing upstairs to pack her remaining belongings.

'It's on me mind and I can't concentrate proper . . .'

'Sit down, please, Mrs. Batt and answer a few questions, after which you can take all the time you need for your packing. I'll try to be brief.'

Winstanley nodded to W.P.C. Blockett, his shorthand-typist, who settled herself to take down the questions and answers.

Mrs. Batt grew impatient right away as her name, age, present address and length of time in Dommett's service were recited to her.

'I've told you that already...'

'Until Mr. Waddilove's sudden death, you, Mr. Dommett, Mr. Bugler and Mr. Waddilove lived here together?'

'Yes. We weren't like a family, though. Mr. Dommett had his meals alone in this room and spent his spare time here as well, just as he and Mrs. Dommett did when she was alive. Me and Mr. Bugler and Mr. Waddilove had our meals in the kitchen and upstairs our separate rooms were furnished like bed-sitters, for privacy if we wanted it.'

'Whatever made all of you stay on in such circumstances? A lonely tumbledown place, remote and miles away from shops and other conveniences. You must have all been bored with your existence.'

Mrs. Batt was indignant.

'I was never bored. There was plenty to do catering and the like for three men, with Mr. Dommett so finicky with his vegetarian food. Where else for a woman of my age would you find work so well paid and I'd my own room and telly to amuse me? Besides, if I wanted to go and shop, or to see my sister, Mr. Dommett always agreed to me going and paid the expenses of my travel, there being very little public transport in these parts. I was comfortable and he treated me like a gentleman.'

'What about the other two, Bugler and Waddilove? Didn't they get restive?'

'I don't know what he paid them, but they seemed well satisfied with what they got. They'd rooms of their own and a telly of their own between them. If either of them wanted a change Mr. Dommett let them off to go to town; separately, of course. One of them had to be here.'

'Did this arrangement meet with Mrs. Dommett's approval when she was alive?'

'She didn't seem to mind it. She was a semi-invalid and didn't go out much. I never talked to him or her about it. She and Mr. Dommett must have agreed about it.'

'Were Bugler and Waddilove with the Dommetts at the other house before you all moved here?'

'Yes. They were there in residence when I arrived . . .'

She suddenly broke off the train of events and spoke to herself.

'I never could think what made Mr. Dommett want to leave his nice house at Slingsby Magna and come and live in a place like this. He might have got short of money, though I never found any evidence of that. He always paid his bills and our wages promptly. You can't say that he came here for the benefit of his health or a bit of peace and quiet for himself. This place is hardly a health resort, is it?'

Winstanley continued his questioning.

'Why do you think Mr. Dommett needed Bugler and Waddilove about the place? What did they do here?'

Mrs. Batt's lips tightened.

'If you ask me, they was like a couple of retired pensioners. I did the cooking and cleaning and they was supposed to look after the property. I'm not surprised that they didn't bother much about the property. This place would need a dozen men to keep it in shape.'

Mrs. Batt was growing anxious about her packing and bored with the questions. She rose and went to the window and looked out.

'I wonder where my sister and Herbert have got to. Still chasing the cat by the looks of it. It'll keep them out of mischief . . .'

She sidled to the door which led to the stairs.

'Just a minute, Mrs. Batt. We haven't finished yet,' said Winstanley. 'We won't be much longer.'

Mrs. Batt flung herself back in her chair petulantly and cast upon W.P.C. Blockett a meaningful feminine look of despair.

'Very well. But I've a lot to do. I haven't made up my mind yet what to wear at the funeral. By the way, when is the funeral?'

'It's not been settled yet.'

'I wish they'd make up their minds. It's not fair to poor Mr. Dommett.'

'Did either Bugler or Waddilove ever stay away overnight?'

'Not to my recollecting. According to what Mr. Bugler once told me, neither of them had any relatives or friends elsewhere, except Mr. Bugler had a sister in London who didn't get on with him. They seemed content with what they were doing here. Having a good old lazy time, with all they wanted for amusement. They went to Aylesdon now and then. Mr. Waddilove would come back smelling strongly of drink and a bit unsteady. Mr. Bugler wasn't like that. I wouldn't be surprised if Mr. Waddilove had got a woman in Aylesdon. He was that sort, if you ask me, although he never treated me with anything but respect. He knew better than try anything on with me.'

'I don't suppose an educated man like Mr. Dommett wanted them about the place for company or conversation. Why, then, did he have them here? As bodyguards?'

'Funny you should say that. I would never have been so forward as to ask Mr. Dommett why he kept them on and spent so much money on it. I knew my place and he would have resented the liberty. But I did wonder if Mr. Dommett was afraid of something.'

'Did it ever strike you that they had some hold over him and were blackmailing him?'

'Blackmailing?'

'Yes. Forcing money out of him by threatening to betray some secret if he didn't give them what they wanted.'

'It might have been. But what sort of a secret was they holding over his head?'

'Your guess is as good as mine, Mrs. Batt. How did Bugler and Waddilove behave towards Mr. Dommett? Were they respectful or familiar?'

'If you ask me, they was familiar . . . They was impudent sometimes.'

'And how did Mr. Dommett react to that?'

'That's what I didn't understand. He didn't seem to mind it. Just overlooked it. I expect he got used to it in time. If I was to have spoken to him in the way they sometimes did he'd have sacked me on the spot.'

'Are you sure?'

'Well . . . He'd have reprimanded me.'

'Was Mr. Dommett afraid of them?'

'You'd have thought sometimes that he was. But Mr. Dommett wasn't the sort to be afraid of the likes of them. I just couldn't understand it, but I had nothing to do with what the three of them thought of one another. I got on with my work and counted my blessings. They never interfered with me.'

Winstanley paused and lit a cigarette.

'Now let's talk about the death of Mr. Waddilove. Tell me what happened.'

Mrs. Batt sighed and tried to look resigned, but her thoughts were evidently on the packing for which she had come all the way to Swinton Lazars.

'About a year ago he had a heart attack. It took him over supper. Terrible pains in his chest, he had. We put him to bed and gave him brandy. Mr. Dommett, when we told him, didn't seem very upset. Just said he'd leave him to me and Mr. B. and if we thought the doctor was needed to send for Dr. Calderwood at Ashby Newbold. Which we did.'

'And then . . .?'

'Dr. Calderwood wanted to have Waddilove moved to Aylesdon hospital, but Waddilove got in such a stew about it and refusing to go that we were afraid he'd have another attack. He said he was better and Dr. Calderwood said very well he'd leave him here for the time being, but on Mr. Waddilove's head be it. He soon got over it. The doctor said it was only a mild attack, but he'd better see that he didn't have another which might finish him. He gave him an injection and two lots of pills; one lot he took regular and the other for use if another attack came on.'

'What became of the pills after Mr. Waddilove died? Did you keep them?'

'A funny thing happened about them. I used to see him taking his daily dose after breakfast. He kept his daily pills on his dressing table and every morning brought one down and put it beside his plate to be took after his meal. It was a sort of capsule. The other tablets he kept in his pocket in case an attack took him when he was away from home.'

'He got over the first attack, then?'

'Yes. Then, one day he came down to breakfast and said he couldn't find his daily pills and had I moved them when I did his room. I said certainly not. I wouldn't think of doing such a thing; he must have misplaced them himself. We hunted about, but couldn't find them. That was on the Tuesday. Mr. Waddilove said he was a lot better and if he hadn't found his pills by Saturday, he'd call at the doctor's and get some more. He had his next attack on the Friday and was dead before the doctor arrived. When the attack started he was shouting for his pills. He took some of the emergency ones, but they wore off and the pain came back worse than ever. The doctor said when he mislaid his daily pills he should have asked him right away for more . . .'

'And he gave the death certificate without an inquest?'

'He talked it over with Mr. Dommett, who'd been a coroner himself, and the doctor seemed satisfied. He said

he'd expected something of the kind as his heart was very
bad and he ought to have been in hospital at the first attack,
but wouldn't go. After the doctor had gone, Mr. Dommett
made us turn out the whole bedroom and all Mr. Waddilove's belonging's to find the lost pills. We found them
under the dressing-table. They must have fell off and rolled
under. It's a wonder we didn't find them the first time we
searched for them.'

'I understand there was a quarrel between Mr. Dommett and Mr. Waddilove just before his fatal attack.'

'Yes. Mr. Waddilove, it seems, had been taking Mr.
Dommett's whisky. There was no need for a row like that.
Mr. Dommett knew very well that Mr. Waddilove helped
himself to his whisky when his own supply ran out. Mr.
Dommett must have been in a bad temper that morning.
He worked himself up into a fine old rage and Mr.
Waddilove, who was hot-tempered, gave as much as he
got.'

'And Mr. Bugler gave his notice and left after the
funeral?'

'Yes.'

'Was there a row about that, too?'

'Funnily enough, there wasn't. I overheard it. They were
both as cool as ice. Mr. B. told Mr. Dommett that he had
killed Mr. Waddilove by getting him so excited in the
quarrel, and Mr. B. wasn't working any more for such an
unpleasant man. I was surprised that Mr. B. was so bold.
He was a timid gentlemanly man and rarely spoke his
mind. Mr. Waddilove was different. An aggressive and out-
spoken man and I can understand Mr. B. leaving when

he hadn't Mr. Waddilove to back him up against Mr.
Dommett.'

Mrs. Batt blinked nervously.

'And now, sir, can I please pack my things and get
away? They seem to have caught the cat and are sitting in
the car waiting for me. Herbert will be getting upset if we
keep him hanging around.'

As though to confirm her statement, Herbert gave a long
blast on the horn of his car. It was a triple affair, like a
small orchestra of cornets, clarinettes and oboes, and
Herbert seemed so pleased with it that he blew it again.

Winstanley turned to Littlejohn, who had been sitting
comfortably in the easiest chair smoking his pipe and listening to the inquisition.

'Have you any questions, Chief Superintendent?'

'You seem to have covered everything. There's just one
matter I'd like to ask Mrs. Batt about. About the anonymous picture-postcards earlier this year.'

Mrs. Batt's troubled face lit up. She had been listening
for a further fanfare from Herbert.

'Oh, those silly things. Very rude, they was, and Mr.
Dommett tore them up.'

'Did they upset him?'

'He was angry when the first one arrived and asked
Mr. B and Mr. Waddilove if they'd sent it. Mr. Waddilove
was impudent about it. He said not to be stupid. How could
they have sent it from the seaside when they was here all
the time? I'd brought the postcard in from the postman
and we was all four here when he arrived. After Mr.
Waddilove had denied knowing anything about it he waited

till Mr. Dommett's back was turned and then he winked at Mr. B. I'm sure they knew something about them even if they hadn't sent them.'

'But why send them at all?'

'I must own up that I read them both on the way. They seemed to be threatening, from somebody who owed Mr. Dommett a bad turn.'

'Did Bugler or Waddilove mention them to you?'

'Mr. Waddilove did pass a remark to me after Mr. Dommett had left the room. "Somebody's cutting the old man down to size from the looks of things. It's given him quite a shock".'

'And when he said that, had he read the postcard or had anybody read it to him?'

'No. I took it from the postman, read it on the way and handed it straight to Mr. Dommett, who tore it up after he'd read it. I don't know how Mr. Waddilove knew about cuttin' Mr. Dommett to size. That was all.'

And she rushed from the room to meet Herbert who was purposefully striding towards the stables to find out what was going on.

9

Coroner's Verdict

DR. CALDERWOOD was the last of a family of doctors who had served the Ashby Newbold district for many generations. At one time the practice had been a busy one, but the decay of the surrounding villages had reduced it to a state which enabled Dr. Calderwood, much to his satisfaction, to combine the pleasures of country life with those of a physician and he spent much of his spare time in hunting and shooting. Until his father's retirement he had been a surgeon in the Navy and he still had a nautical freshness and bearing.

When Littlejohn arrived at the charming stone house from which the doctor practised, he was just about to start out on a round of professional visits and his horse was standing ready in the cobbled yard behind. Dr. Calderwood, when the weather permitted, frequently combined business with pleasure, cantering from patient to patient in the good old-fashioned way.

There was a modest plate on the gate: *Dr. J. C. Calderwood,* and as Littlejohn made his way up the garden path a handsome woman wearing an old straw hat and with her hands hidden in formidable gardening gloves called to him from behind the rose bush she was clipping.

'Do you wish to see the doctor? You're only just in time. He is just ready to do his rounds.'

Littlejohn introduced himself and the doctor's wife shook hands with him.

'I suppose you're calling about Mr. Dommett's death. A sorry business. Hunting for clues in that old ruin must be a fresh experience even for you. Come inside and make yourself at home. I'll find the doctor.'

The room was indeed pleasant, with comfortable chairs and kindly old furniture, a few excellent water-colours on the walls and Persian rugs on the polished floor. The doctor hurried in and made Littlejohn welcome. He was a medium-built, robust man, whose kindly courteous manner was doubtless often worth more than a dose of medicine to his patients.

'Take a seat, Chief Superintendent. What would you like to drink?'

And when the drinks were ready they settled down to business.

'My wife tells me you are here on the Dommett affair. Old Dommett must have been important to merit the attentions of Scotland Yard.'

'Was he your patient, doctor?'

'No. From what I gather, Dommett was the type who despised medicine and doctors in the same way that he had no time for religion and parsons. Dr. Carter, of Aylesdon, attended his wife during her last illness. My father, in his early years, was doctor to the Mowll family, who owned Swinton manor, but since then the connection has lapsed.'

'You did, however, deal with Waddilove, who lived at the manor with Dommett, doctor. I don't know how to describe Waddilove's occupation. Manservant? Security Guard? Attendant? I don't know . . .'

'I was going to mention Waddilove. It was a peculiar set-up. He and the little fellow Bugler were like a couple of pensioners there. As far as I could gather, they were a pair of hangers-on. What claim they had on Dommett's charity – if such it was – I never found out. Waddilove became my patient by accident.'

'Accident?'

'Yes. Dr. Carter, of Aylesdon, was the family doctor when one was needed. He was absent on holidays when Waddilove had his first heart attack and I was standing in for him. When he returned Dr. Carter should have taken over the case, but he asked me to carry on, as he and Dommett had quarrelled at the time of Mrs. Dommett's death and Dr. Carter didn't wish to encounter him again. Dommet, as you doubtless know, had a reputation for quarrelling with everyone with whom he came in contact. Did you know him?'

'Yes; and I agree with Dr. Carter. When he was a county coroner I encountered him on several cases and found him most unpleasant, especially after his daughter eloped with a police constable.'

Dr. Calderwood had a good laugh at the idea.

'I never heard about that! It reminds one of a theatrical farce!'

'And to add fuel to the fire, when the policeman died, she married again, and her husband this time was a doctor, the son of Dommett's partner in a legal practice who absconded with the partnership funds and was sent to gaol. I believe Dommett was responsible for his partner's downfall. The doctor and his wife are, I think, living in Toronto, where he is in practice . . . So you inherited Waddilove?'

'What a tangle of intrigue the whole business is. Yes; I took on Waddilove. He was an alcoholic and in very poor shape when I first saw him. He'd had a coronary and might easily have died. They didn't send for me until he'd passed the worst. They filled him with brandy. He made a quick recovery, refused to go to hospital and challenged my diagnosis. He said he'd had dyspepsia. But I hadn't much hope for his future. He apparently didn't take any notice of my advice, especially about cutting out alcohol altogether.'

'You gave him medicine to take regularly?'

'Yes. I prescribed an anti-coagulant to keep his blood in condition and some trinitrin capsules to relieve him should he have any further spasms. He had two later attacks; the second was a massive one and he died before I got to him.'

'You were able to certify death from natural causes?'

There was an embarrassed pause and the doctor lost some of his cordiality.

'Is there something I ought to know about this murder case? I feel I might be becoming involved,' he said sharply.

'Not at all, doctor. This Dommett murder has become so complicated that every avenue has to be explored. There is a mystery about the presence of Waddilove and Bugler in the Dommett family and I'm seeking as much information as I can about them.'

'Well, I can certainly answer your last question in the affirmative. Of course I could certify death as being from natural causes. In other words, there was no reason whatever for an inquest. From the beginning Waddilove's heart was in a shocking state and he did nothing to improve the condition. A post-mortem would have shown death due to coronary thrombosis.'

'Did you know that for several days before his death Waddilove was not taking the pills you prescribed for daily use?'

The doctor did not seem very surprised.

'I told you, Littlejohn, that I did not expect him to follow my advice, although I underlined the necessity for taking those pills, as his life depended on them. He was a stupid fellow and thought he knew better than I did. Who told you this?'

'Mrs. Batt, the housekeeper. She told me he took the pills quite conscientiously until he mislaid them and they were not recovered until after his death. They were subsequently found under his dressing-table where they had presumably fallen and rolled there.'

'How long was he without them?'

'As far as I can gather, about three or four days. He told Mrs. Batt he intended to call in and ask you for a fresh supply.'

'Four days! That was enough to restore the blood to its unhealthy condition. What are we to think of this?'

' I'm beginning to think Waddilove was deprived of the pills deliberately.'

' I saw Dommett before issuing a certificate of death. He assured me that Waddilove had continued my treatment right to the end. Dommett behaved like a typical coroner. A lot of frigid talk, like a summing-up in his court. He stated categorically that death was due to natural causes. Had I not thought from the previous prognosis that such was the case I would have ordered a post-mortem. I had no idea that Waddilove had been deliberately deprived of the pills. Dommett lied to me.'

There was a pause.

' What do we do now, Littlejohn?'

Dr. Calderwood was troubled and he said so.

' You were not to blame, doctor. Death was due to natural causes. But it might have been delayed if Waddilove had taken the pills. It seems to me that someone deliberately concealed the daily pills. . . . Wait! Dommett must have done it. He told you the pills were taken right to the end. How did he know? Mrs. Batt told me he took little interest in Waddilove's illness. I must speak to Bugler about this. Meanwhile, do not worry about your part of the affair. You were perfectly regular in your handling of the case. You did not know that there was a murderer loose at the manor house. Leave the matter in my hands and I'll keep you informed about developments.'

' I seem to have told you all I know, except the clinical details, which are technical . . .'

' There is one final point. Did Dommett, when you discussed Waddilove's death, mention to you that he and

Waddilove had quarrelled fiercely just before his final seizure?'

'He did not. Had he done so I certainly would have remembered it. What was it all about?'

'Dommett rebuked Waddilove about drinking his whisky. According to Mrs. Batt it seemed a paltry matter to start a row about, especially as Dommett knew that in the past Waddilove had regularly helped himself to his drinks.'

'I had particularly told Waddilove to take things easy and not in any way to agitate himself. A quarrel like the one you mention might easily have triggered off the final seizure. Dommett must surely have known that from his professional experience.'

Littlejohn rose to go and the doctor saw him to the door.

'I'm very grateful to you, doctor, for all your help,' Littlejohn said as they parted. 'I'll keep in touch and let you know what happens. Meanwhile, as I'm here in Ashby Newbold, I may as well call at the bank . . .'

'There's only one in the place and it's a sub-office to Aylesdon. I don't think you'll get much help from Pomfret, the clerk in charge. He's a nervous chap and he'll probably fob you off to the main office when he finds you're from the police. You will have to hurry if you wish to see him today. It's three o'clock and the bank closes at 3.30.'

They shook hands and, as Littlejohn turned to go, he was surprised to see Grimes passing the gate. He was dressed in his best suit of battered navy blue serge and wore an old bowler hat. He was evidently enjoying a day off in town and as he strolled along he was eating what appeared to be a large meringue.

Littlejohn turned back to the doctor.

'Did you see the man who just passed the gate, doctor?'

'You mean Grimes?'

'Yes.'

'He's what you might describe as a casual patient of mine. About a year ago he had a wound in the thumb which turned septic. Mrs. Batt, Dommett's housekeeper, telephoned and fixed an appointment for him with me here. I dressed the thumb and gave him a tetanus injection and he came two or three times. Meanwhile, I grew interested in his deafness. I persuaded him to let me examine him. I cleared a lot of debris from both his ears and then sent him to the hospital at Midchester, where they eventually fitted him with an ear-aid. His joy at hearing again was pathetic . . .'

'The rascal!' said Littlejohn. 'As one of the inhabitants of the Swinton manor estate we have had to interrogate him. All the time he never once mentioned he had an ear-aid. Our questions have either been shouted at him without much success, or written down for him and where he didn't wish to reply he pretended he couldn't read the writing.'

'I was going to say, he is very crafty about the ear-aid. People have probably been used to him being stone deaf and said many things in his presence which he could not hear. This they continued to do, I guess, unless they knew of his contraption. When he found the police in the vicinity he must have kept his ear-aid in the dark and hidden behind his infirmity. He got an excellent instrument through the hospital. It cost more than the usual standard model, which he managed to engineer by a show of pathetic ignorance and a grant from a local charity.'

'I must have another talk with Grimes; this time with the assistance of his contraption, as you call it, doctor . . .'

'Be careful in your approach, then. Come upon him when he's got his ear-aid in his ear. Otherwise, if he knows you're from the police, I guess you'll have a long preamble of bawling and writing getting him to produce it. The only bus back to Swinton for him leaves here at five o'clock and meanwhile you'll find him in the square watching all the girls go by and eating sugary confections from the pastrycook's.'

'Thanks again, doctor, for all your help. And now I'll see what Mr. Pomfret has to say.'

Littlejohn hurriedly crossed the road to the picturesque branch of Garfitt's Bank, comfortably established in what had once been the priest's house. As he entered he met the junior clerk on his way to the front door to close for the day. He looked impudently at his watch and then at the electric clock in the banking hall. There was a staff of three: Mr. Pomfret; a young lady who, judging from the speed with which she was counting banknotes, combined beauty with efficiency; and Rothwell, the junior, who that evening was playing in a football match and resented Littlejohn's late arrival which probably would cause a delay in his programme.

Mr. Pomfret was counting notes as well. When Littlejohn, a stranger to him, entered, he swept the money from the counter into a drawer out of sight and looked ready to defend his cash with his life. Meanwhile, the pretty young lady continued to count her notes with remarkable rapidity and sang froid. She had bigger fish to fry than worrying about a possible bank raid; she was meeting her boy-friend in an hour's time and they were going all the way to Midchester to choose an engagement ring.

Mr. Pomfret was a tall, thin, nervous man of between 30 and 40 with buck teeth. He was not much of a banker and the placid business of Ashby Newbold was quite enough for him. After all, he had a nice wife, his father was wealthy and young Pomfret would inherit the lot when he died, and to this he added the tennis championship of Ashby and district. What more could he want? His nervous tendency was due to the fact that he himself had once been the centre of a bank raid in the large Midchester branch of Garfitts, when a man with a nylon stocking over his head and face had shot at him with a revolver. Luckily, the man had been a poor shot, and ran into the arms of a policeman on his way out. Mr. Pomfret had been consigned to a quieter branch to recover his nerve after his ordeal. He was sent to Ashby Newbold and had remained there ever since.

With one foot poised over the stud in the floor which operated an alarm system of bells and flashing lights in the street and rang bells in the neighbouring police station, Mr. Pomfret asked Littlejohn what he could do for him. He sighed with relief when he read the warrant card which Littlejohn passed across the counter.

'How much did you want, sir?' said Mr. Pomfret, thinking that Littlejohn was stranded and wished to reveal his identity and cash a cheque.

Littlejohn explained the purpose of his visit, whereupon Mr. Pomfret invited him into his private room. This, judging from its size, might have been the hole in which the priest hid when the roundheads were about. It harboured piles of old financial papers, banking journals and text-books, and packets of stationery. There was a desk there with a chair on each of two sides of it and at Mr. Pomfret's suggestion Littlejohn took the one obviously allocated to clients. On the wall opposite him was the photograph of a past chairman of the bank, which someone had forgotten to remove.

'Mr. Dommett banked with you, I believe, Mr. Pomfret.'

Mr. Pomfret seemed to think that Littlejohn was getting along too fast. The police, before they arrested a man, cautioned him, and Mr. Pomfret thought it only fair that a banker should do the same.

'You do understand, Chief Superintendent, that everything between banker and customer is strictly confidential. . .'

He looked across at the shelf of technical banking books, wondering if Littlejohn was going to ask for chapter and verse.

'Of course, I understand that, Mr. Pomfret. But in this case the customer was murdered and the police are asking you to co-operate in the investigation . . .'

Mr. Pomfret nodded sagely.

'I quite understand. I'm sure my head office would agree . . .'

Mr. Pomfret didn't know whether they would or not, but he didn't care much because his father-in-law was a big shareholder in the bank and would get him out of any trouble.

'What kind of an account did Mr. Dommett keep with you?'

'Just a personal current account. He used it for the usual household expenses and the wages of his staff. Now and then he drew out fairly large sums in cash when he had bills to pay in connection with his property. I always said it was throwing good money after bad. Have you seen his property at Swinton? An old ruin of a manor house and a lot of tumbledown old out-buildings. He lived in the stables, which he'd converted into living quarters.'

'Did he carry a large credit balance?'

'His income came from a few scattered investments, but the main source was from large annuities. The annuity payments came half-yearly in January and July. When those amounts were received his credit balance was a good one, roughly £4,000. But it was gradually whittled away by expenditure and sometimes he'd be a bit over-drawn until his next annuity payment came in. He also had his pension paid direct to us. It was a small one, about £800 per annum. He hadn't been a coroner very long. I believe he was in his own law practice before that.'

'Can you give me some details of his expenditure?'

'Yes. I think I could do that. But first, do you mind waiting for a few minutes while I lock up and let the staff go? I believe they have appointments and I'd better see them off . . .'

Which was very considerate of him, Littlejohn thought.

Pomfret was not long away and returned carrying some large loose ledger sheets which turned out to be the records of Dommett's account.

'You know, of course, sir, that the Bank is Mr. Dommett's trustee,' said Pomfret as he sorted out his papers. 'I was one of the witnesses to his will.'

'Do you think he will leave much?'

'I'm telling you this, sir, in strictest confidence and with the view to saving you trouble . . .'

'I appreciate that, Mr. Pomfret, and if we wish to use any of the information you are volunteering I'll see that proper legal authority is obtained for it.'

'Well . . . I don't think Dommett will leave much. You see, the large annuities will be extinguished by his death. He had already realised most of his other investments. As for the value of his property, it is a bunch of ruins and nobody wants to build out there, so the land isn't worth much either.'

'Did you say he drew large sums from his account to pay for repairs and improvements to his property?'

'That's what he said when he made withdrawals of any size. He was always complaining and when he drew out the cash he invariably grumbled about the expense of keeping up the property.'

'Why didn't he pay by cheque?'

'I don't know sir. He was a queer fellow. I wondered if he paid cash so that he could deduct discount when he came to pay.'

'Do you know who did those jobs for him?'

'I've no idea. If I'd asked him he'd have been sure to tell me to mind my own business. He quarrelled with everyone.'

'Did he call here regularly for his money?'

'Once a month on the last Friday.'

'You say you have details of his account, Mr. Pomfret?'

'Yes.'

'Could you tell me then, what was the annual turnover?'

'£5,000 approximately, last year. This year, at the rate he was spending, it would be nearer £6,000.'

'Increasing cost of living?'

'Probably. It has gradually risen year by year. Soon his expenditure will exceed his income.'

'And now, what about the cash drawings. How much did he withdraw monthly?'

Pomfret consulted the account sheets.

'Roughly £200 monthly. Then, of course, there were the quarterly withdrawals for the repairs and expenses of the estate.'

Pomfret totted up more figures.

'Roughly about £2,000 yearly.'

'All in cash?'

'Yes.'

Pomfret busied himself with his figures, whispering to himself as he jotted them down.

'This year, if he goes on as he is doing . . . or *was* doing, I'd forgotten he was dead . . . his cash will have risen from £2,000 to £3,000. Cost of living, I guess. But he was getting out of his depth. At that rate, he'd be over-spent and would have to economise. He hadn't many investments to sell . . .'

'By the way, Mr. Pomfret, would it be possible for you to tell me about the will of which your bank is trustee?'

Pomfret hesitated and thought for a minute.

'It is very private, you know. But I might just give you a hint, seeing that it will soon be made public. In the new will, he left all he had to Mrs. Batt, his housekeeper. Which will not be very much, as I said before. His money was mainly in annuities which died with him. A few investments and, I guess, the property, for what it is worth, and that won't be much I can assure you.'

'You say the new will. Had he recently changed it?'

'Yes. Less than a month ago. He brought it in here. Being a lawyer, he'd drawn it up himself and two of us here witnessed it.'

'Who was the beneficiary under the old will.'

'There were three of them; Mrs. Batt, and his two manservants, if such you could call them, Bugler and Waddilove. It was changed just after the death of Waddilove.'

'Did you know Bugler and Waddilove?'

'Not very well. They didn't bank with us.'

'Where did they keep their accounts?'

'I really don't know. Waddilove had been in the army and drew a small pension. I used to cash the warrant for him. That's all.'

Pomfret glanced anxiously at the clock when he thought

Littlejohn was not looking. Time to go, thought Littlejohn.

Outside, the main street was crowded with visitors. The
bus from Ashby Newbold to Aylesdon through Swinton
Lazars ran only twice weekly, Thursdays and Saturdays,
gathering in shoppers and villagers on outings from the
neighbourhood in the morning and returning at five in the
afternoon. Littlejohn strolled casually along, hoping to
find Grimes somewhere among the visitors. The High
Street held shops, antique dealers, butcher, baker and con-
fectioner, two or three clothing boutiques, and an over-
sized ironmonger's with a spread of all things needed by
amateur gardeners. The street widened at the end into a
village green with a duckpond and a bus shelter in bad
taste. Littlejohn found Grimes on an empty seat there.
He was eating Cornish pasties with enthusiasm.

Grimes must have spotted Littlejohn as soon as he appeared on the scene. He fumbled on the side of his face,
furtively removed what must have been his ear-aid, and
slipped it in his jacket pocket. Then he raised his head and
nodded at Littlejohn.

' Waiting for the bus?' said Littlejohn.

There was no reply. Grimes had entered into his silent
world again.

Littlejohn took an envelope from his pocket and scribbled
on it and passed it to Grimes.

*I want a private talk with you. Put your ear-aid back,
or else I'll have to take you in the police station.*

Grimes gave him an alarmed look and cast his eyes round
the crowded green. Then at the police station next door to

the ironmonger's. There was a small car labelled POLICE at the door and beside it P.C. John Fancy, the local bobby, was surveying his kingdom.

Grimes lost his customary hesitancy, took out and set up his listening contraption reluctantly, and gave tongue.

'Mr. Dommett wouldn't like it,' he said, as though it was still a charm against all intrusion.

10

Four Hundred Pounds

LITTLEJOHN and Grimes sat side by side saying nothing for quite a long time. Littlejohn filled his pipe and began to smoke and Grimes returned to his Cornish pasties, rapidly consuming them one after another, like an elephant with a bag of buns.

Grimes had been used to living in the private world of his own and was not yet accustomed to being sociable and making conversation. Having eaten the main parts of his pasties he tore open the bag and carefully picked up the crumbs of the feast on his forefinger and sucked them. Next, he opened another bag, took from it a large meringue and buried his face in it. Then the bus arrived. Grimes slowly wiped his face, shook himself down and prepared to join the queue which was forming.

'No need to trouble yourself about the bus, Grimes. I'm going to Swinton myself and you can join me in the car.'

Grimes seemed delighted and resumed his seat in the bus shelter. Littlejohn sat beside him.

'You like your new ear-aid, Grimes?'

Grimes was non-committal.

'It be all right . . .'

'You can answer some questions, then?'

Grimes made no reply.

'Tell me where you found Mr. Dommett's gun which the policeman caught you digging up in the garden.'

Grimes remained dumb, staring ahead, his body bent and his hands between his knees.

'Are you going to answer me here, Grimes, or are we going to the police station . . . ?'

Grimes looked across the green to where P.C. Fancy was still taking the air.

'Here,' he said laconically.

'Well?'

'Mr. Dommett gave it to me. "Grimes," he said. "I have no more use for a gun at my age. I'll give it to you " . . .'

There was a pause as Grimes gathered his thoughts together.

' " But " he says, " But . . . you must hide it," he says. " You not having a licence, you will get into trouble with the police. Hide it till I get a licence for you." So I wrapped it in an old oilskin I had and buried it in the garden, as suggested by Mr. Dommett.'

'You say Mr. Dommett suggested that you should bury it in the garden?'

'He did that. I thought it would have been better in the house, but Mr. Dommett said the garden was the best place, so be it.'

'Now, Grimes, do you swear that you're telling me the truth about this?'

'Why should I tell a lie about it? The policeman saw me

dig it up. It was my gun, Mr. Dommett having given it to me. That's no lie.'

'When was this?'

'The day before Mr. Dommett died.'

'But why should anybody suggest hiding a fine gun in the garden? Do you know what that gun is worth?'

Grimes thought about it. 'Ten pounds, maybe.'

'Four hundred.'

'Cor!' said Grimes gutturally. 'That be a lot of money. Why would he give me a gun like that? Will the police give it me back?'

'Yes, in time. Did anyone else know Mr. Dommett had given it to you?'

'I dunno. He didn't say. But when I get it back I shan't hide it in the ground. Will the police give me a licence so I can use it?'

'I guess they will. Have you a gun of your own?'

'Yes. But I don't use him much. Mr. Pepperdy, in the village, gave him to me. The hammer is a bit tricky. It isn't safe to anybody but me. I know how to use him.'

'Now, Grimes, you're telling me the truth?'

'Gospel truth. I wouldn't tell a lie about a £400 gun. You're sure I'll get it back?'

'Yes.'

'With a £400 gun, the rabbits and partridges and rats . . . maybe it's too good for rats. Four hundred pounds!' He said the last three words slowly.

All the way back to Swinton Lazars they said very little, but now and then Grimes exclaimed to himself 'Four . . . hundred . . . pounds!'

They found Winstanley and two of his staff at the manor busily going through the drawers in Dommett's desk and dressing-room.

'There's nothing here of much help,' said Winstanley.

Littlejohn told him the story of Grimes's gun. Winstanley was flabbergasted.

'Had Dommett gone mad? £400! Why give a gun of that type to an oaf like Grimes?'

'Why indeed? Dommett wasn't the kind who gave away such costly articles. He had something very much in mind. Suppose he wanted to get someone out of the way and clear himself of suspicion. He gives Grimes the gun and tells him to bury it, pending his taking out a licence for Grimes. He checks that Grimes has buried the gun, digs it up, shoots his victim, and then buries the gun again. In the subsequent inquiry he tells the police that someone has stolen the gun and the weapon is found in the garden bearing Grimes's fingerprints. In Grimes, Dommett thinks he has chosen the ideal scapegoat. Slow, half-witted, deaf and easily provoked. He is so confused in his mind that under questioning he would probably incriminate himself. As for the gun, who would give away a gun of that kind to a peasant like Grimes? Dommett, the skilled advocate, an ex-coroner used to inquiries of that type, would be believed and the stammering Grimes would be the culprit.'

'Quite a good theory. But Grimes had an alibi for the crime concerned. He was at Cold Barsby. Dommett would know he was going there . . .'

'He didn't. He'd forbidden Grimes to go. And Dommett knew, or thought he knew, that his orders to Grimes were obeyed without argument. He forgot that the fair was an annual event and part of Grimes's annual routine. Grimes disobeyed him this time.'

'If this proves to be the case, it was a dirty trick to saddle Jason Grimes with murder.'

'Characteristically Dommett. He thought of nobody but himself and his devices. I guess he thought poor Grimes a disposable half-wit and fit to be sacrificed to save his own skin.'

'The lab people report that the gun bore the prints of Grimes, but that would naturally be due to his handling it when he dug it up. Nothing more.'

'By the way, was Dommett's daughter informed of his death?'

'Yes. We telephoned the Toronto police and killed two birds with one stone. We asked them to tell Imogen Dommett – now Gutteridge – about her father's death and, at the same time, check that she and her husband were in Canada at the time of Dommett's death. I thought Dr. Gutteridge might perhaps have borne a grudge against his father-in-law for Dommett's share in his father's ruin. Both Dr. Gutteridge and his wife haven't been away from Toronto for quite a while. Gutteridge is a prominent surgeon and his movements were not hard to follow.'

Littlejohn knocked out his pipe on the heel of his shoe.

'Speaking of Gutteridge's father reminds me, we ought to go more fully into the embezzlement case,' he said. 'If you agree, and would like me to see our Fraud Squad about it, I'll do so. Commander Flight, the head, is a good friend of mine and can probably dig up details in his records. It must have been quite a famous case and even if Scotland Yard wasn't involved in it they'll have it classified in the archives.'

So, Littlejohn found himself back in London enjoying a lunch at Simpson's with Commander Flight.

Horace Flight was a tall, thin, melancholy-looking man, who always shed his sadness when facing a memorable meal. He seemed to associate Littlejohn with good food and often when they were on a case together their business was transacted over a meal. Littlejohn had telephoned him from Swinton and posted him concerning the Dommett affair.

'That crackpot!' he said when Dommett's name was mentioned. 'I met him a time or two in the course of duty. What's he been up to now?'

'He's got himself murdered!'

'I'm not surprised! I've a vague recollection of the Gutteridge case. Wasn't Dommett mainly responsible for Gutteridge's downfall?'

'That's right. I wonder if our present case might have some roots in the past, especially in the Gutteridge affair.'

'I'll look into it and let you know. Will you be in London tomorrow?'

'Yes.'

'What about lunch . . .?'

And when they met, Flight, who had no notes or files with him, was a complete master of the details of the case.

'Gutteridge had been living above his income for many years and trying to straighten out his affairs by unsuccess-

ful speculation and seems to have made up his deficit by pil-
fering from some inert trusts in his care as a lawyer. He kept
up the income payments to beneficiaries whilst eroding the
capital for his own purposes. In all, the fraud involved about
£50,000. He was bound to be caught sooner or later, but
probably hoped for the best, which never came.'

' I believe it was his partner, Dommett, who finally discovered the misappropriation.'

' Yes. Poor Gutteridge must have lived in hell for many
years. Sooner or later, the whole sorry business would
explode and land him in gaol. He never knew when it
would occur and even dispensed with holidays lest in his
absence someone came upon the crime and disclosed it.
All his efforts came to nothing, for he had an accident and
was confined to hospital for a short while, during which
Dommett, exploring in the firm's accounts, discovered the
fraud and blew the whole thing sky-high.'

' It would have to be Dommett, wouldn't it?'

' In the cool light of logic, what else could Dommett do?
He'd a perfect right to access to the firm's affairs and once
he'd found out what was happening was bound to report
his findings to the proper quarter.'

' One ought not to sympathise with Gutteridge, Horace,
but somehow, it would have been less unsavoury if Dommett hadn't been involved in it.'

' He got a lot of credit from it for his astuteness and skill.
But there was one aspect of the case which was discounted
at the time and which, now that the heat is off and the
matter can be regarded objectively, seems important. Gutteridge eventually confessed and made a statement. But he

insisted that the £50,000 was a miscalculation and that £40,000 was nearer the mark. He died in gaol and to his last day alive persisted in challenging the amount.'

'It might have been an obsession or maybe he was frightened by the extent of his crime.'

'It might also have been true, and in that case, *two* of them had been indulging in the fraud. Perhaps quite unknown to each other, or perhaps together.'

'And yet, Gutteridge didn't disclose the name of the second party – his confederate?'

'He never mentioned him. It is doubtful if the idea ever entered his head. He simply seems to have thought that there was an error in the accountant's check of his defalcations. At the time it must have been easy to think he was beside himself and that his crime and its subsequent discovery and his total disgrace and ruin had affected his mind. There the matter rested.'

Flight produced some cigars and they started to smoke them. From the amount of time he took to cut the cigars, sniff approvingly at his own and then methodically light it, Littlejohn judged that Flight was holding up his story for a dramatic finale.

'Gutteridge's method of manipulating the accounts was quite simple. He and another party, Mountford, also, until his death, a partner in Gutteridge & Dommett, had been made trustees of the eccentric estate of Ethel Alice Helliwell Fink, deceased. Mountford had died and Gutteridge neglected to have another trustee appointed. The total capital of the trust was about £200,000 and the income was distributed among relatives. It was in the nature of what is known as a tontine, whereby the beneficiaries share the income, and as each dies the shares become proportionately larger per survivor, until all the capital eventually devolves on the last one.'

'That's a new one to me,' said Littlejohn.

'Tontines were quite fashionable at one time . . .'

Flight paused as an opulent-looking man smoking a large cigar greeted him and passed on.

'That was Godwit,' he told Littlejohn. 'Out of gaol three months and, judging from his appearance, is up to his old tricks . . . where were we?"

'Tontines.'

'Gutteridge did not, of course, sell the lot of the capital. Now and then, as required, he changed some of the investments, selling, let us say, £10,000 worth and buying £5,000 worth; he kept the balance for his own purposes, which included making the periodic payments to the beneficiaries. This went on for a few years, with Gutteridge tight-roping his uncertain way to destruction. He was a clever lawyer and avoided many pitfalls skilfully until his crime caught up with him. It only needed one of the beneficiaries under the trust to ask for information about it or scent irregularity for the whole affair to be brought to the light of day. As it was, nobody bothered. They all received their periodic dues promptly, Gutteridge's integrity was assumed, and the merry-go-round continued until Dommett thrust his finger in the pie.'

'Was the amount of the defalcation covered by insurance?'

'Yes; the usual indemnity. The company paid up.'

'I suppose Gutteridge opened an account at another bank for his illegal transactions.'

'Yes. He ran an account at a merchant bank, Merganser and Prewitt. That was easily traced. Gutteridge paid in at Merganser's the proceeds of the stock sales he had appropriated. It was impossible to handle them without a bank account.'

Flight paused and called for more drink.

'I'm almost at the end of this unhappy tale. It was at the Merganser's end that the Fraud Squad had most trouble. They assisted us to the full in our inquiries, but there was a cheque on Gutteridge's account that was missing. It was for £5,000. In common with most banking practice, paid cheques are forwarded by the bank to the customers who drew them, after the bank has dealt with them, and all Gutteridge's cheques on Merganser's were sent back to him after payment. Gutteridge kept these cheques in a locked box in his private safe. One would think he'd have destroyed them, but in his methodical way he retained them. Three months before his crime was discovered Gutteridge had drawn a cheque for £5,000, in cash. He frequently drew large amounts in cash, saying they covered property deals. The cheque was never found. Merganser's swore they had returned it to Gutteridge after payment; Gutteridge never even remembered the transaction. In his state of mind he seemed to have lost all contact with reality. As you know, he died in gaol, a mental and physical wreck. Eventually the Fraud Squad and the partnership accountant decided the cheque was irrevocably lost. It didn't really matter; the bank had their records in their accounts and the Fraud Squad decided to take them as proof of the item.'

'And there the matter rested?'

'Not quite, Tom.'

'Well?'

'Let's regard what follows as fiction. First, Dommett and Gutteridge, the partners, working in adjacent rooms, sharing information, probably understanding one another's moods. Dommett was quite a clever fellow, if an awkward and unsociable one. He noticed a change in Gutteridge. His partner grew furtive and on edge. He seemed to spend a lot of money and perhaps Dommett discovered that he was speculating heavily on the Stock Exchange and also kept a private account at another bank. Even if he never asked Gutteridge what was afoot, Dommett must have been burning with curiosity. Especially when Gutteridge, afraid something might turn up to betray him, abandoned his annual holidays and remained working at the office. Of course, Dommett could have faced Gutteridge and demanded an explanation, but he wasn't built that way. Instead, he managed to get hold of his partner's keys and took an impression and had copies made of those of Gutteridge's private safe. Then one day, back alone at the office, he opened the safe and found out what Gutteridge was doing.'

'You've got a good imagination, Horace. By the way, Gutteridge was married, wasn't he? I ask because I wonder what his wife had to say about no holidays . . .'

'His wife had died before all this. As for my imagination, we need it in the Fraud Squad! We might embellish this fiction and add that Gutteridge was keeping an expensive woman! However, to continue our flight of fancy, Dommett at the time he opened the safe was either greedy or hard-up. There, in the papers of the safe, was the whole sorry story, including a statement of Gutteridge's account at Merganser's Bank, showing a credit balance of over £5,000. Dommett, the enterprising burglar, saw an original and easy way of blackmail. He forged Gutteridge's signature on one of the cheques in the cheque book there, drawing £5,000. Gutteridge, if and when he discovered the item, daren't create a hullabaloo about it; he was too afraid of an inquiry which would bring his felonious little game to light.'

'Dommett surely didn't go and cash the cheque himself! He daren't!'

'He could have asked the bank over the telephone to send the money by messenger. Among our files on the case there is a list of Merganser's staff from top to bottom. They had three messengers, Renshaw, Andrews and Waddilove . . .'

Littlejohn could hardly believe his ears!

'Waddilove!'

'Yes; Wilberforce Waddilove. He delivered the cash to Dommett; Merganser's was just round the corner from Dommett and Gutteridge's office and the bank frequently sent letters by hand to neighbouring clients. The letters were all entered in a book and the messenger who delivered them signed for them. We inspected that book. There were three such letters delivered to Dommett and Gutteridge at the time and it is likely that one contained the cash and, a day or two later, another containing the paid cheques, including the one forged by Dommett. A confederate in the lawyers' office got hold of that.'

'Now we are beginning to see daylight, Horace,' said Littlejohn. 'We have two likely suspects, because Bugler was on Dommett and Gutteridge's staff. Either Bugler at the lawyers' office, or Willy Waddilove at the bank had his suspicions aroused when he found Dommett handling cash from Gutteridge's account. And that started the whole sorry business. What you said was fiction is now becoming reality. Imagine Dommett's agony when he found that the cheque he'd forged and was anxious to get back and destroy, had vanished into thin air.'

II

The Second Gun

THE FOLLOWING morning Littlejohn made the journey to Midchester by train and Winstanley met him there and they travelled to Swinton Lazars by road.

Although Littlejohn had briefly informed him by telephone of Flight's information and theories, Winstanley, delighted at the turn of events, insisted on hearing the story all over again.

'This is a very interesting and involved case, Tom. Do you really think Dommett was being blackmailed by his two muscle-men and had made up his mind to murder them both?'

'Flight said he was only making up fiction from the facts before us, but I'm sure he felt we were getting near the truth. What astonishes me is the two cases of blackmail. Somehow, it seems, a trio of men, Bugler and the two Waddiloves, got hold of the cheque drawn by Dommett on Gutteridge's account at Merganser's. This was a forgery and could, by experts, have been confirmed as such. That would have put Dommett in gaol as well as his partner.'

'Dommett seems to have had plenty of luck, doesn't he? Although he lost the incriminating cheque, the police and the accountants did not make heavy weather of it, and accepted the bank's assurance that the transaction was legitimate. And Gutteridge's condition after his arrest. Overwhelmed by his guilt and resigned to his punishment, he doesn't seem to have made much of an outcry about the alien cheque. Had he been in his right mind and aggressive enough, he could probably have convinced the police of the crime within a crime and led them to Dommett.'

'There's a dramatic side to the case, too, Frank. Dommett, having forged his cheque and acquired his £5,000, finds that he has also landed himself with a couple of rogues for life! If Willy Waddilove was also a party to the blackmail he must have taken a cash payment and left Harold Waddilove and Bugler to arrange their board, lodging, spending money and leisure with Dommett, who must have been so scared of the crime being made public that he took them as part of his domestic establishment. And he had to invent yarns and subterfuges to explain the situation.'

'Finally, he must have grown tired of it all and decided to put an end to it . . .'

'I think the reason was financial. He must have been sick of the sight of the pair of them and they must have felt the same about him. But cost of living was rising and the bulk of Dommett's money was locked fast in annuities, which he couldn't turn into cash and which yielded only the same income however much the cost of living rose. His account at Garfitt's Bank showed considerable fluctuations. A moderate amount of cash in hand when the annuity income arrived at regular intervals and then smaller amounts as the money was spent, ending up sometimes as an overdraft. Now and then he drew substantial sums in cash, which he said was to pay the expenses of keeping up the estate. Knowing the nature of the estate, we are sure that wasn't true. It was cash down to keep his tormentors quiet. There they were, living lives of ease and he couldn't do a thing about it. Finally, he decided to do away with the pair of them and concocted a plan which almost succeeded, but ended in his death.'

' What exactly was Dommett planning, Tom?'

' Waddilove's heart attack played right into Dommett's hands. As a coroner, he must have dealt with scores of cases of sudden death from thrombosis. He knew of the existence of anti-coagulant medicines, and finding that Waddilove was under such treatment he hid the tablets, and involved Waddilove in a violent quarrel which gave him a heart attack, from which, having been denied his medicine for several days, Waddilove died.'

'Bugler must have guessed what had happened and was afraid violent death was intended for him, too. He packed up and left.'

'That's right. Whatever fate Dommett held in store for Bugler had to be shelved and a new way of disposing of him arranged. Dommett hatched his little plot, it didn't come off, and he was hoist with his own petard. He gave Grimes his own gun and persuaded him to bury it until he could obtain a licence for him. Grimes, obedient to the letter about Dommett's instructions, did so. Then, Dommett was all set for bringing Bugler back and shooting him and leaving Grimes, stupid, incoherent and bewildered, to take the blame.'

'But Dommett would need another gun to kill Bugler.'

'That is one of the gaps in the theory. We must find out if he possessed another gun. The coast was clear, Mrs. Batt was in town, but Grimes, unknown to Dommett, had sneaked off to Cold Barsby fair and given himself a cast iron alibi. And, unfortunately for Dommett's complicated plot, Bugler didn't turn up! His sister gave him an alibi. He was in Wimbledon at the time Dommett died. Also, the second gun was never found; so, presumably if our creaking theory is true, the murderer took it with him.'

'So we've still a lot to do before we reach the winning post?'

'Yes...'

They were back at Swinton Lazars. In the courtyard shone Herbert Tidy's elegant motor-car and the owner was standing, with a companion, in the midst of the ruins of the manor house. As soon as he saw the police he nudged the other man, indicated the officers and both of them scrambled from among the tumbledown wreckage and hastened to meet them.

Both men were dressed in black and wore bowler hats and each held a brief-case. They were obviously present on business.

Herbert could not even wait to greet them.

'The bank has informed Mrs. Batt that she's the sole legatee of the late Mr. Sebastian Dommett...'

'So they told me,' said Littlejohn.

Herbert looked very disappointed and annoyed.

'Why the bank should inform the police I can't think. But that's as may be. This is Mr. Bluett. He's a valuer who'll take charge of selling the whole place, as Mrs. Batt refuses to live here . . .'

Mr. Bluett, a tall fat man, breathing heavily from his exertions, shook hands with the two policemen and said he was pleased to meet them. He must have been an optimist if he expected to sell the ruins that surrounded him.

'We won't disturb you, gentlemen,' said Littlejohn. 'Is Mrs. Batt here?'

'She's in the house, deciding what she'll retain and what she'll sell. I'll come with you.'

'Don't trouble, Mr. Tidy. Continue with your deliberations,' said Littlejohn pompously, falling in with Mr. Tidy's attitude. 'We'll see you later.'

Mr. Bluett, for some reason, seemed eager to get away from the police and made off for the ruins again and Herbert reluctantly followed him.

Mrs. Batt was in the dining-room busily putting labels on the furniture, some of which were marked 'Keep' and others 'Sell'. She was dressed in black mourning for Dommett from head to foot and tried to greet them solemnly although she was delighted with her good fortune.

'You've heard the news,' she said. 'Poor Mr. Dommett. I didn't expect this. I'll never forget his kindness. I can't believe it.'

And she licked one of her labels marked 'Sell' and slapped it on the top of the huge dining-table which looked as if it would require the removal of one of the walls to get it out.

'When is the funeral to be?' whispered Mrs. Batt. 'There will be a funeral, won't there?'

'Yes. We'll let you know as soon as the police have finished their investigations.'

Mrs. Batt looked alarmed.

'What are they investigating? Are they cutting poor Mr. Dommett's body up?'

'Let's leave that for the time being. You know, of course, that Mr. Dommett gave his gun to Grimes before he died?'

Mrs. Batt looked annoyed.

'Yes. I do. He told me he'd given it to Grimes and to bear witness to it. Of course, having given my word, I can't go back on it. Mr. Dommett might haunt me if I did. It was Mr. Dommett's best gun, too, and worth a lot of money. I wondered if Grimes would change it for the other one...'

'Had Mr. Dommett two guns, then?'

'Yes. But I can't find the other one. That's gone as well.'

'Did Mr. Dommett use both guns?'

'No. The one he gave to Grimes was the one he used. He bought it cheap in an auction sale at Grisby Hall and used it ever after. The other was put away in the attic but it's gone. It was there last time I was in the attic a fortnight ago ... It's all a mystery to me. Do you think I ought to tell the police?'

'We are the police...'

'So you are. I am sorry. You two don't look like policemen. Two nice gentlemen, you are . . . Did you see my brother-in-law and Mr. Bluett on your way in?'

'Yes. They were exploring the ruins of the manor house.'

'They want me to sell it and I am agreeable. I could never live here. It's an unlucky place. A place of ill-repute, as Mr. Gradeley used to say.'

'Who's Mr. Gradeley?'

'He was curate here. Very interested in old ruins. He used to lecture on them at Women's Institutes. He was made vicar at Flecking Harcourt and there hasn't been a curate here since.'

She looked through the window anxiously.

'I do wish Herbert wouldn't keep wandering about in the old manor house. It's dangerous. A lot of the stone is loose. Mr. Bugler was nearly killed once by a fall of stone. It just missed him.'

'When was that?'

'I remember it well. It was just before Mr. Waddilove had his first attack.'

Winstanley gave Littlejohn a knowing look. The first move in Dommett's offensive against his two blackmailers? Or *was* it the first?

Mrs. Batt stuck a label marked 'Keep' on a grand-father clock.

'Did Mr. Dommett keep any record of his cases, Mrs. Batt?' asked Littlejohn. 'You know what I mean: Coroner's Court records.'

Mrs. Batt paused in her contemplation of a rocking-chair which had seen better days.

'Mr. Dommett's favourite chair,' she said. 'He was a

great one for rocking. He'd sit there, thinking, and rocking up and down till you thought he'd make himself seasick. And he got quite cross if anybody disturbed his thoughts. I was never a rocker myself. I'll sell the chair . . . Was you asking something?'

' Did Mr. Dommett keep any records or diaries of his court cases?'

' He burned them all when he moved here. He said he never wanted reminding of courts and the law again. It was something about his pension, I think. They didn't give him enough, from what I gathered, although he never took me into his confidence about it. But he was in such a temper and shouted about the house. He said he ought have more for the cost of living. But those responsible didn't seem to agree with him.'

' You remember Mr. Dommett writing to me about wishing to meet me. You said you thought he was going to offer me a house, similar to this one, which he was thinking of constructing next door.'

' Yes. I remember. He thought you were going to retire very soon and might like it.'

' Anything more?'

' You would be company for him, too. After Mr. Waddilove died and Mr. Bugler left Mr. Dommett and me were on our own here. I wouldn't have left him alone, but I did mention that we could do with somebody handy about the place. You never know what happens nowadays. With the hooligans and gispies about, we might all be murdered in our beds. And look at what happened to poor Mr. Dommett. It wasn't right living on our own.'

'But what did he think I would do in my leisure even if we did move in here?'

'He didn't say. But now that I know you, sir, I'm sure it wouldn't have suited you or your wife. It was a servant's job and not one for a gentleman.'

'Did Mr. Bugler and Mr. Waddilove regard themselves as servants?'

'They did not. You'd have thought they owned the place. How Mr. Dommett put up with them for so long I can't think. Mr. Bugler was all right when that Waddilove wasn't about. But Waddilove was the ringleader and egged on Mr. Bugler all the time. He was a common man, was Waddilove. No wonder Mr. Dommett having rid himself of the pair of them, wanted a nice educated gentleman as a neighbour.'

'Do you recollect the offensive post-cards that came for Mr. Dommett?'

'Yes. He tore them up in a temper, but never found out who sent them. You see, Mr. Bugler and Waddilove were here when they came and they couldn't have sent them. Although I'm sure Waddilove knew more about them than he let on. He winked at Mr. Bugler as if it was a joke while Mr. Dommett was going-on about them, but when he and Mr. Bugler were alone in their sitting-room I heard Waddilove very angry about something. I was up there doing my own room and overheard Waddilove saying "The fool! What did he do that for? It won't do him any good . . ." Something like that. They might not have been talking about the post-cards at all, but as it was just after the first card came it might easily have been that that caused Waddilove to go on so.'

It might have been true. On the other hand, it might have been a silly red-herring.

Mrs. Batt paused in her chatter and looked at the clock.

' It's nearly dinner-time, sirs. Would you care to have a meal here if you're staying on duty? I've got some eggs and could make you an omelette.'

They thanked her and said that would be very nice. As Littlejohn was proposing to call on Bugler again that afternoon it was very convenient, too.

The luncheon might have been spoiled by Herbert and Mr. Oscar Bluett, who appeared on the scene, pompous and breathing heavily from their exertions, but Herbert quickly put them at their ease.

' Mr. Bluett and me are just off for a bite of food at the *Dun Cow*,' he said. ' See you later.'

And they made off without asking the police to join them.

' Well, I never,' said Mrs. Batt angrily.

She was paying Herbert's expenses for his so-called services and, as the *Dun Cow* was the most fashionable and expensive restaurant for miles around it didn't seem fair.

The Phantom Cheque

MRS. FLOWERDEW, Bugler's sister, was indignant when Littlejohn turned up at the house in Wimbledon again.

'Can't you leave him alone?' she said in reply to Littlejohn's greeting. 'Being mixed up with the police – which he's never been before in his life – is making him ill. He's off his food and he can't sleep. Every night I can hear him tossing and turning and his bed creaking . . .'

'May I have a word with you before I see him again? There's a matter I wish to check.'

Mrs. Flowerdew looked anxiously up and down the street. 'You'd better come in the front room then. I don't want the neighbours talking.'

She led him through the first door on the right in the lobby. The room was obviously little used and reminded Littlejohn of a jumble sale. An out-of-date suite in American leather, little bamboo tables, a threadbare carpet and the damp smell of disuse, a mixture of soot and dry rot. Scattered around, china objects of all shapes and sizes, plant pots, tureens and small souvenirs with 'A present from Margate' and 'A souvenir from Bournemouth' inscribed on them. Articles of clothing hung over the backs of chairs.

Mrs. Flowerdew made no excuses for the room and its contents. She got down to business right away.

'What is it?'

Littlejohn mentioned the date of Dommett's death.

'Where was your brother all that day?'

A lock of Mrs. Flowerdew's lank hair dislodged itself and fell over one eye. She flung it back angrily.

'Why don't you ask him?'

'I have done so. He says he was here all day. Is that so?'

'Don't you believe him? He's not a liar, you know . . .'

'Mrs. Flowerdew, if you'll just answer my questions we will end this interview and I'll get on with my business with your brother.'

Her lips tightened.

'Very well then. He was here all day.'

'Are you sure?'

'Of course. I remember it. As a matter of fact, he and I had a row about him always getting under my feet about the house. He doesn't go out enough and I can't get on with my housework for him always being in the way. I complained to Mrs. Matthias about him . . .'

'Who's Mrs. Matthias?'

'Next-door neighbour on the right. She's a district nurse. So, perhaps you'll believe her if you don't believe me. She came in here twice that day and saw Reginald both times.'

'Was that the day Mr. Dommett died?'

'Of course. That's the day we're talking about, isn't it? The day Mr. Dommett passed on . . .'

Mrs. Flowerdew was a spiritualist, saw apparitions and believed in the Bugler ghost, which warned the family of the 'passing on' of any member. Littlejohn had once had an aunt of a similar frame of mind and was thus able to deal sympathetically with Mrs. Flowerdew. She ended by reassuring Littlejohn that all was well with Reginald according to her divining spirits, the principal one of which was the late Mr. Flowerdew. Nevertheless, Littlejohn thought it best to interview Reginald in the flesh.

Bugler, whatever his condition in bed, was asleep in his chair when Littlejohn entered. His sister shook him awake and he whimpered as he opened his eyes.

' You frightened me!' he told her.

' The police is here again.'

Bugler quickly recovered consciousness.

' What is it?' he asked Littlejohn apprehensively.

Mrs. Flowerdew showed no curiosity about the nature of this new interview.

' I've the dinner to get ready and you'll be shouting the odds if you've to wait for it,' she told her brother and left them with a slam of the door.

' You'll have to excuse her, Mr. Littlejohn. She's 'ighly strung. What do you want now?'

Bugler didn't look at all well. His complexion was a pale liverish yellow and his cheeks were puffy and lined. He was obviously under some strain.

' Have you found out who did for pore Mr. Dommett?'

' We're well on the way. It won't be long before we make an arrest.'

' Was it Grimes? He's not *compos mentis*, you know.

You never know what he'll do next. He did some funny things when I was at Swinton.'

'No; Grimes has a perfect alibi. I'd like to tell you what we've discovered so far and you can correct me as we go along . . .'

Bugler grew taut with anxiety, but made a show of giving Littlejohn the closest attention.

'You were managing clerk to Dommett and Gutteridge before the partnership ended?'

'That's right. And when it broke up, I became a coroner's clerk to Mr. Dommett.'

'And you remained with him until a few weeks before his death.'

'Yes.'

'Why?'

'I was out of a job and Mr. Dommett made me an offer, which I gladly accepted. I saw no reason for changing it.'

'Not even after Mr. Dommett retired?'

'I was due to retire about the same time. I had no home of my own, having lived in single furnished rooms most of my life. It seemed a good idea to become what one might call the steward of Mr. Dommett's property.'

'Even before Mrs. Dommett inherited it?'

Bugler blinked nervously. Littlejohn could imagine his mind furiously working to concoct an answer.

'There were many things to clear up after Mr. Dommett's retirement and as his home was in a large house he offered me lodging there and I continued as his right-hand man until he went to Swinton Lazars.'

'What about Waddilove? He accompanied you in these various changes and removals.'

'He was originally one of the messengers of the Coroner's Court. Mr. Dommett was impressed by his diligence and invited him to join his staff. When we retired, Waddilove was what you might call my deputy . . .'

'One wouldn't think a deputy was required for a job like yours. There was, as far as I could gather during the investigations, not enough work for even one man.'

Mr. Bugler raised a restraining hand.

'Ah, Chief Superintendent, there were other reasons. I think I told you that violence was anathema to Mr. Dommett. He found it abhorrent. You know he was once assaulted by young Gutteridge and it almost broke him up. After that he felt he needed protection.'

'Even after young Gutteridge died?'

Bugler struggled mentally for another excuse.

'There were other reasons we never knew, Chief Superintendent. He was afraid of something, which to my thinking eventually led to his awful death.'

Littlejohn felt he had suffered quite enough from Bugler's flights of imagination.

'Shall I tell you what our investigations have revealed, Mr. Bugler? Something very different from the rambling account you have just given.'

Bugler began to perspire visibly and his face twitched with a nervous tic, presumably due to the strain of recent events and his sleepless nights.

'You know, don't you, that the frauds at Dommett and Gutteridge's brought the Fraud Squad from Scotland Yard into the case? Their records tell a very different tale from yours . . .'

Bugler sank down in his chair, his mouth fell open and his eyes protruded. His hand fumbled for the bottle and glass on the table at his side and he poured himself a stiff drink. Littlejohn did not interfere. In the circumstances a stimulant seemed appropriate. The drink appeared to have little effect. Bugler trembled as he waited for the worst.

'Before the defalcations of Gutteridge were exposed by Mr. Dommett he was already aware of them and took the advantage of joining in the frauds. He drew a cheque on Gutteridge's private account for £5,000, forged Gutteridge's signature on it and cashed it. Then, when he thought it appropriate, he blew the frauds wide open. Even if Gutteridge knew of the illegal cheque what could he do? Expose it and bring down his own illicit behaviour? He kept quiet. Even after his arrest he said nothing about it, for he might not have known who drew it, and was too confused to pursue the inquiry in any case. Dommett got away with it, as he was sure he would. But not quite.'

Bugler stretched out his hand as though to stop the narrative, but Littlejohn continued.

'Where is that cheque, Mr. Bugler?'

'I don't know what you mean? I know nothing about the cheque.'

'If you do, you'd better tell me right away. Otherwise, you are going to find it hard to avoid a harrowing inquiry into the conduct of yourself and Waddilove since you took up with Dommett. That cheque has been a means of blackmailing Dommett for years. It explains your living on his bounty ever since you obtained it. You are going to fall foul of the Fraud Squad, of whose efficiency you are already well aware . . . And to add to blackmail you have murder. You know that Dommett in the end, hounded to despair by the pair of you, virtually murdered Waddilove. And you were to be the next. Only you got the blow in first and killed Dommett . . .'

Bugler suddenly became active. He rose to his feet, tottered a few steps and seemed about to make a run for it. He looked at Littlejohn, then at the window and then at the door. And gave it up. Instead he stood over Little-john and raised his right hand, as perhaps he used to do in court.

'I swear that I had nothing whatsoever to do with the murders of Sebastian Dommett or Harold Waddilove and that the felonious cheque for £5,000 has never been in my possession. So help me God.'

And as though the oath had cost him all his strength, he collapsed on the hearthrug.

Littlejohn gave him another stiff dose of whisky and had half-a-mind to call his sister and leave Bugler in her care. But this time the drink revived him and he scrambled to his feet and slumped in his chair. He chattered as if to himself.

'I have known no peace since I got involved in Waddi-love's schemes. No peace or sleep. Only remorse . . .'

It was like a scene in a melodrama. Littlejohn put an end to it.

'Let us get down to business. Where is that cheque?'

'I don't know. Waddilove had it. I searched his belongings after his death but I couldn't find it. He must have hidden it somewhere.'

'Now you needn't be afraid to bring the ringleader of this affair to light. Has Willy Waddilove got it?'

At the mention of Willy, Bugler showed signs of panic again.

'It was Willy Waddilove who started this blackmail business by means of the forged cheque, wasn't it, Mr. Bugler? He was a messenger in Merganser's, a small merchant bank with whom Gutteridge kept an account for his secret illegal transactions. Somehow Willy Waddilove became aware of the £5,000 withdrawal in which Dommett, not Gutteridge, was involved. He suspected something irregular and probably mentioned it to his brother, Harold. I suspect that neither of the Waddiloves was bright enough to engineer what followed and you, Mr. Bugler, were brought into the affair.'

There was a silence whilst Bugler racked his brain for another excuse for his position.

'Imagine my 'orror,' he said, 'When approached by Harold Waddilove. He came and laid a cheque on my desk and said "That's a forged cheque drawn on Mr. Gutteridge's account by Mr. Dommett." I couldn't believe it. And when Waddilove explained how he had come by the cheque, through his brother, who had extracted it from a bundle of paid cheques drawn by Mr. Gutteridge on Merganser's Bank, which as bank messenger Willy Waddilove had been instructed to hand to Mr. Dommett and not to Mr. Gutteridge, I thought I was having a nightmare.'

'How could you be sure it was forged?'

'Willy Waddilove had a friend in the Tottenham Court Road who was an expert in handwriting. It wasn't difficult to obtain a specimen of Mr. Dommett's writing from our office for comparison.'

'Who was this expert?'

'I think his name was Alexander. He was a pawnbroker.'

'I know. He was a fence and served five years after we nailed him. He was a handwriting expert, too, and a clever forger. Continue, Mr. Bugler.'

'He said Gutteridge's signature was indeed a forgery, although quite a good one. Judging from the way Mr. Dommett accepted the situation, Mr. Alexander was right.'

'How did Dommett react?'

'I do assure you, Mr. Littlejohn, I was not a party to the arrangements made by the Waddilove brothers. I merely knew of the forgery and they did the rest.'

'You compounded a felony, Mr. Bugler, and well you know it.'

'What else could I do? Willy Waddilove was – and is – a desperate, violent man. He threatened me. I was in fear for my life . . .'

'Let us leave your emotions. Dommett, I suppose, dared not tell the three of you to go to hell and take the consequences. He had never anticipated encountering a trio such as the three of you and he had to make the best of a bad job . . .'

'You are hard and unkind, Mr. Littlejohn. I cannot convince you of the peril of my position.'

'At the best, you were a coward, and at the worst, a rogue.'

Mrs. Flowerdew appeared and reminded her brother that dinner was growing cold.

'Go away! Can't you see I'm busy,' yelled Bugler with unusual energy.

'I *beg* your pardon, Reginald!'

'Go away!'

Mrs. Flowerdew thereupon withdrew and slammed the door with such vigour that it dislodged the portrait of their musical father from over the fireplace and it fell with a crash in the hearth.

'Where's that come from?' shouted Bugler distractedly as though he'd never seen it before.

'I think you'll be lunching at Scotland Yard today, Mr. Bugler, so let's get on with the story . . . Now, let us discuss the arrangements you and your accomplices made with Mr. Dommett and then his subsequent murder.'

'You're not arresting me, are you? I'm innocent and can prove it.'

'You'll be given a chance to do that. We'll need a full statement from you. After the forged cheque had appeared and, so to speak, you had Dommett and your money, what happened? Who kept the cheque?'

'Harold Waddilove did a bit of photography as a hobby. He photographed the cheque and they produced a photo of it to Mr. Dommett. It was, according to what Harold said – I wasn't present – like a coroner's inquiry. Mr. Dommett sat in judgement on Willy and Harold and questioned and bullied them. But it was no use; they had the cheque certified by an expert as forged and Mr. Dommett knew it. The only thing that kept them on tenterhooks all the time was what Mr. Gutteridge would do when he found out about the missing £5,000. But nothing happened. Come to think of it, what could Gutteridge have done? If he'd taken any proceedings the whole of his crimes would have been brought to light. Somehow or other, in his confused state of mind – he was, for a time completely out of his mind – the matter was overlooked. And instead, Mr. Dommett, with his usual effrontery, exposed what I'm sure he'd known long before that, Mr. Gutteridge's swindles.'

'Who was responsible for the novel arrangement of Dommett paying blackmail by giving you and Harold Waddilove board and lodging in his home?'

'It was arranged between the Waddiloves and Mr. Dommett and I fell in with it. I think it was Harold's idea. He'd read about such an arrangement somewhere in a book. Mr. Dommett agreed to me and Harold, but he refused to have Willy anywhere near him. As I said, Willy was vulgar and violent and Mr. Dommett said he'd rather go to gaol than tolerate him under his roof. So Willy was paid a lump sum and Harold and I became part of Dommett's domestic staff and drew good wages and lived in. Now and then Willy tried putting on the screw. Mr. Dommett said he couldn't afford any more lump sums, so Harold and me had to pay Willy off. It was a satisfactory state of affairs; we lived well and had little to do.'

'It was a most amazing set-up. However did Dommett manage to tolerate it?'

There was a pause.

'Judging from what has recently happened, I think that one day he planned to kill us all. But Willy kept his distance, took his money and drank like a fish. He's an alcoholic.'

'I know that. How did you avoid being murdered?'

'We were on the premises and I suppose Dommett was afraid that Willy, from his convenient distance, would betray him if anything happened to Harold and me. So Mr. Dommett had to wait his chance. It came at last when Harold had his heart attack. I guess Dommett was disappointed when he recovered, so he took the risk of hiding his medicine and starting a furious quarrel with Harold, which brought on the attack that killed him. I was sure my turn would be next, so I left the place as soon as possible.'

'And you haven't been back to Swinton since?'

'No. I told you I hadn't and my sister will confirm that I was here when Dommett was killed.'

'Why have you been so eager to tell me all this? As a rule statements to the police aren't easy to come by.'

Bugler seemed surprised.

'I told you to convince you that I haven't, all along, been guilty of a crime. I was a sort of sleeping partner compelled to go along with the rest out of sheer compulsion.'

Sheer compulsion! That was a good one!

'You forget, Mr. Bugler, that you have, all along, at least compounded a felony.'

'But I can turn Queen's evidence and it wouldn't go hard with me then.'

'That remains to be seen. Whatever happened between you, Dommett was brutally murdered. Not by the doubtful removal of his heart pills, but clubbed to death. You state you have your sister's alibi. That may have been arranged between you ...'

Bugler beat the arms of his chair in rage.

'It's a lie! We wouldn't do such a thing. I've told you the truth. What more do you want?'

'The whole truth. Did Dommett send for you after you left Swinton?'

Bugler hesitated, then made up his mind.

'Yes. He telephone to say he wished to see me to settle our affairs, as he called it ...'

'But you aren't on the phone, are you?'

'We use the telephone next door. She's a district nurse and when I was living at Swinton Lazars Dommett knew he could contact my sister there in case of emergency.'

'Did he fix an appointment?'

'Yes. He as good as ordered me to be there at noon on the day he died.'

'And you didn't go?'

'No. I didn't.'

'You were afraid of him?'

'I didn't know what he might do if I got there. I'm not much good at that sort of thing with a domineering man like Dommett. You called me a coward. You can call me anything you like. I was afraid.'

'Was there any good reason for you going to Swinton to square matters up?'

'Dommett owed me £100 for back wages and I'd left

some odds and ends behind. I was in such a hurry to get away after Harold's death that I forgot things.'

' So you got in touch with Willy Waddilove?'

Bugler sat upright and sighed heavily.

' How did you know?'

' It's obvious. You knew Willy was a match for Dommett and would collect the money for a share of it. Have you seen him since Dommett's death?'

' No, I haven't. I don't expect him. He has probably got the money and other things and doesn't intend to turn them over. I ought never to have got in touch with him.'

' Do you know that Dommett had arranged to kill you if you went to Swinton?'

Bugler languished in his chair as though he was still in peril.

' It's a nightmare! I wish I'd never seen Dommett or the Waddiloves. I guess Willy is planning to kill me now. Whatever shall I do?'

' You can come with me to Scotland Yard. And put a few things in a bag. You'll perhaps be staying with us for quite a time.'

*   *   *

With Mr. Bugler lodged at Scotland Yard, Littlejohn, accompanied by two other detectives, hurried off to the Waldstein Hotel in Paddington. There, by arrangement, two more constables awaited them, one discreetly watching the front and the other the rear of the hotel.

The front door was open, but when Littlejohn and Detective Sergeant Hopkinson entered Mrs. Cuffright immediately descended on them from her private room. She looked pale and resigned, still fighting to make at least a living out of the place in spite of its uncertain future and clientele.

'Are you here again? I really must protest. The coming and going of the police gives the hotel a bad name and I have had enough to worry me without this. What is it this time?'

She spoke in a flat monotone as though too despondent even to open her mouth properly.

'May we speak in private, Mrs. Cuffright?'

She indicated the first door on the left and ushered them in. A small shabby room which once must have been the residents' lounge. Worn armchairs scattered about, a threadbare carpet on the floor, an ancient television set neglected in one corner and shelves on each side of the fireplace with old bound copies of *Punch* and the *Strand* magazine spread along them. She did not offer them chairs.

'Please be brief. I am alone at present; the staff are taking time off just now.'

Littlejohn got the impression that this little charade of being full up was a pathetic part of her stock-in-trade.

'Is Mr. Waddilove at home?'

'Yes. He hasn't been out all day.'

'Is he still employed?'

'I don't know. He seems to flit from job to job. Never keeps one employment for long.'

'Does he pay regularly?'

'Yes. I have to ask him frequently to pay his bill, but he never seems short of money. He meets his accounts from a wallet full of notes.'

'Is he what you would call a desirable lodger?'

'No. He is not a very good client, but he pays and seems content with where he is. I could well do without him, but with this compulsory order over my head I am glad to keep any clients I can put up with.'

She paused, wondering what it was all about.

'Why? Has he committed a crime? Is it about Miss Munroe?'

'What about her?'

'After your last visit she packed her bags and went. They had a noisy quarrel and he even struck her. She had a black eye when she left. He threw her bag down the stairs after her and used the most outrageous language. He was drunk, of course. He quite upset the other guests. I left him to quieten down and sober up and then I asked him to leave. He apologised most contritely, paid his own bill and that of Miss Monroe, and gave me £5 for the damage. He had smashed a chair and scattered a plant-pot in the hearth. Is he in trouble for assaulting Miss Monroe?'

'No. We have some questions to ask him. Perhaps we'd better go up to see him. But, first, you may be able to help us . . .'

He gave her the date of Dommett's death.

'Do you happen to remember if Mr. Waddilove was out during that day. I understand he slept during the mornings after night-watching in the West End. I know it's a difficult question, but perhaps you'll recollect something . . .'

Mrs. Cuffright suddenly became animated. She did not even need to ponder the question.

'I certainly remember that day. Contrary to his usual practice, Mr. Waddilove returned from his night work in a hired car and went off for the day. When he returned late in the afternoon, he approached me and informed me candidly that he had been in trouble with the police, a mere nothing involving speeding, and had evaded the police car. He asked that should the police call here to inquire, would I inform them that there must be some mistake as he had been indoors here all day. I refused flatly and he grew quite offensive and used bad language.'

'Thank you very much, Mrs. Cuffright. That is most helpful.'

Up the stairs again to what had once been the servants' quarters, with the shabby carpet yielding to linoleum at the first floor. The doors were both closed and Littlejohn knocked on Waddilove's. There was a scuffling within and then Willy's voice.

'Who is it?'

'The police.'

'What do you want?'

'Open up. We've some questions we want to ask?'

There was a pause, as Willy considered the situation. Then he turned the key and let them in.

He was as soiled and seedy as when last they met. His braces hung down and he had an old pair of slippers on his feet. He was not yet drunk, but there was a bottle on the table with which he would shortly, if allowed, soon finish the job.

Waddilove was indignant at the intrusion. He said so in flowery language.

'. . . A man has a right to be left alone without the police always banging on the door.'

'We'll come to the point right away, Mr. Waddilove. It seems you were off gallivanting in a hired car on the day Sebastian Dommett died. Where did you go?'

'Who told you that? The Cuffright woman? You can't believe anything she says.'

'But you were out in a hired car . . .'

Willy Waddilove's neck grew red and a flush slowly rose in his face. He was keeping his temper with a struggle.

'Anything wrong with that? A man has a right to some fresh air and a change of scene now and then.'

'Of course. I trust you found Swinton Lazars salubrious enough.'

'Where's that? Never heard of it.'

'But you were there and you met Dommett, too. And you then tried to bully Mrs. Cuffright into concocting a phoney alibi by saying you were here all day.'

'I asked her that because I got chased for speeding by a panda car and managed to shake him off. I ought not to have asked Cuffright to cover for me with an alibi. I was wrong there and I'm prepared to own up and pay my fine.'

'You told me a pack of lies when last I was here. You got Cora Munroe to give you an alibi. Did you threaten to black her eye then? I hear you did it later.'

'She was too fresh. Thought she owned me . . .'

'You lied about your relationship with your brother, Harold, and Bugler too. You said you rarely saw Harold, didn't know Bugler and weren't on good terms with either of them. Actually, you were on very good terms with both. You were the leader of the little gang which for years black-mailed Sebastian Dommett . . .'

Willy addressed himself to Detective Sergeant Hopkinson.

'Hark at him,' he said. 'All I've done is dodge the police for speeding. I've confessed and here he is, piling crime after crime on me. I think I'd better get a lawyer.'

'We're not joking, Waddilove. This is serious and it concerns the murder of Dommett who you went to interview on behalf of Bugler, who funked facing him again . . .'

'Who told you that rubbish?'

'We are holding Bugler at Scotland Yard and he has made a statement.'

Waddilove exploded.

'Has that little swine grassed on me? He's a liar . . .'

'Everybody's a liar but you, Waddilove. We know all about your days at Merganser's and your stealing a forged cheque, which you held over Dommett's head until he finally turned to murder to free himself. You knew Dommett was virtually the cause of your brother's death. Where is the cheque?'

For an instant Waddilove seemed to remember something he'd forgotten. Then he was himself again.

'What cheque? I don't know anything about any cheque. If that's what Bugler told you he's a . . .'

'He's a liar. They're all liars.'

'If they're trying to shop me, that's what they are. I know nothing about blackmailing Dommett.'

'You'll have to tell the Fraud Squad about that. They

investigated the Dommett and Gutteridge fraud and have all the details. I suppose they are liars as well. I'll tell you what *we* know. Dommett having got one of his tormentors, your brother, out of the way, laid a plan to eliminate Bugler. But Bugler, being almost a witness to your brother's murder, was scared to death and gave Dommett a wide berth. He sent you to collect his debts and belongings. You and Dommett met and quarrelled and instead of killing Bugler, he got himself killed. You killed him, Waddilove. There were only three of you in this affair. Your brother was dead and Bugler has a cast-iron alibi. That leaves you, Waddilove, and you are coming with us to Scotland Yard to answer more questions and, if necessary, to argue your case with Reginald Bugler.'

' Are you saying you're arresting me for murder?'

' You are accompanying us to Scotland Yard to assist us in our inquiries.'

' I know what that means. And I'm not coming and you can't make me . . .'

Waddilove boiled over and began to rave like a madman.

' I tell you you can prove nothing and you're not taking me in for a third degree at Scotland Yard. You're not pinning this on me.'

' Calm yourself, Waddilove. If you can prove your innocence you'll be free to go afterwards . . .'

' I tell you I know what will happen. You'll try to pin it on me. I'm not coming and you can't make me.'

Hopkinson moved across the room and stood with his back to the door. Waddilove rose and moved equally quickly to the bottom drawer of the rickety wardrobe. He fumbled among a lot of clothes and turned before Littlejohn reached him. He had a shotgun in his hands.

'Stand back, Littlejohn, or I'll blow a hole in you – and you, young fellow, stand away from the door.'

'You can't get away with that, Waddilove. The place is surrounded by police. Besides, the gun isn't loaded. Is it the one you took from Dommett? You made a mistake there. You ought to have disposed of it right away.'

'Don't try anything. It's loaded as you'll find out if you move any nearer. I kept the gun just in case something like this happened.'

Hopkinson looked like standing his ground.

'Don't resist him, Hopkinson. Let him go. We don't want more police widows.'

Hopkinson stood aside and Waddilove backed his way through the doorway, took the key and locked the door after him.

'Careful now, Hopkinson. Don't take any risks.'

Hopkinson stood on one leg and kicked the door open.

Fire regulations being what they were, a small flight of steps from one corner of the landing led to a trap-door in the roof. Waddilove had obviously escaped that way.

Hopkinson leaned over the banister and blew his whistle. A small squad of policemen began to ascend the stairs. Various lodgers, alarmed by the noise which had been going on above, gathered on the landings below and in the hall. Mrs. Cuffright stood wringing her hands and excitedly talking to a reporter who had materialised from somewhere, while an attendant photographer took her photograph.

FRACAS IN PADDINGTON HOTEL
' I knew he was a scoundrel' says owner.

Littlejohn and Hopkinson climbed to the top of the small stairs and cautiously peeped out. The roof ran a confused course along the terrace of large houses. Here and there pipes and projections appeared among the trapdoors and ramshackle mansards. Waddilove might have been concealed behind any of them. Littlejohn and Hopkinson scrambled gingerly on the roof and two policemen from the squad below joined them.

' Be careful,' shouted Littlejohn. 'He's armed.'

None of them had weapons; they had not expected this. They fanned out, seeking cover behind the projections. Waddilove was nowhere in sight.

For some reason, the last two houses of the terrace had been extended upwards by brick erections, making a further series of rooms with sloping slated roofs, the lattter accessible by a rusty iron inspection ladder. Waddilove suddenly broke cover and, finding himself trapped, climbed the ladder and steadied himself on the slates. Then he moved his gun in a semi-circle as he viewed his pursuers and shouted down at them.

' Stay where you are or I'll shoot.'

He looked cautiously around for a final line of retreat.

As he did so, Hopkinson crouched and ran from one of the mansards to behind a large chimney stack ahead. Waddilove lost his head and fired. Hopkinson found cover just in time and there was a crash of breaking glass as the shots hit one of the skylights.

The gun either kicked or Waddilove's perch was insecure. He cut a strange caper like a soldier eccentrically marking time as he tried to regain his balance, lost it, flung his arms in the air, slid down the roof and vanished over the side. As he fell, the second barrel of the gun went off.

In the side street below, two men inspecting the electric cables had erected an object like a tent over a manhole and Waddilove fell spread-eagled on top of it. The men, who had surfaced for some fresh air and a smoke, seeing a row of policemen's helmets looking down at them from above, decided to detain Waddilove who struggled feebly to get away but had been reduced to bottom-gear by his fall. As he battled with the larger of the two electricity men he suddenly ceased his struggles and confided in him. ' It was manslaughter,' he said and lost consciousness.

' I thought at first he was an acrobat,' said the electrician when next morning his wife proudly showed him his picture in the paper.

The gun fired by Waddilove was examined and although it seemed to have been superficially cleaned, traces of blood and hair, which tallied with those of Dommett, were found. It had evidently been used to batter Dommett to death after Waddilove had disarmed him. In any case Mrs. Batt identified the weapon as belonging to Dommett. She regularly wiped it over when she cleaned the attic where it was stored.

Waddilove, on the advice of his counsel, changed his plea to manslaughter. Dommett had attacked him and he had defended himself. Dommett had expected Bugler to arrive and when, instead, the aggressive Waddilove had appeared, a quarrel had developed arising out of Dommett's usual cantankerousness and had ended in violence and threats.

There ensued a strange trial in which Bugler showed that he had not forgotten the law. The blackmail arising from the forged cheque was aired. Counsel for the defence pooh-poohed the 'phantom cheque', denied its existence and watered down the cause of the death of Sebastian Dommett to a violent brawl between him and Waddilove about Bugler's belongings. The Merganser's partners had died and the business had been dissolved long ago. No details were available from that source and the Fraud Squad records were not precise enough.

On the fourth day of the trial, closely reported by the press and labelled 'The Phantom Cheque Case', Littlejohn received a letter addressed to 'Mr. Littlejohn, Scotland Yard, London,' the envelope postmarked Dublin, with no address and no date.

Dear Mr. Littlejohn,

I have been reading in the newspaper about the case of the fantom cheque and because of your kindness to me when we met in Padington I am sending the enclosed. It was given to me by W. Waddilove when very drunk just after you left. Keep this for luck he said, it's no good now. He never asked for it back as I think he too drunk to remember what he done with it. Hope you are well as it leaves me at present. Thank you again Mr. Littlejohn.

                                        Cora Munroe.

Enclosed was the soiled forged cheque for £5,000 drawn by Dommett on the account of Gutteridge at Merganser's. Willy Waddilove got ten years and Bugler got three.